For my mother,
who has been waiting patiently for me to finish this.

THE AUTHENTICITY INITIATIVE
Cari Lyn Jones
TOOK THE PLEDGE

Cari Lyn Jones

The Seven Sisters' Fairytales

Lapis Moon Publishing

Acknowledgements

To Rackham, Dulac, Outhwaite, Globe, and Tarrant; to Lang and Pyle; to all the golden age illustrators and story gatherers who sparked my imagination and inspired in me a sense of wonder and a love of fairytales…

To all of you on Kickstarter, who brought this book to life. Especially Kate, whose sharing and enthusiasm (though I believe she called it "obsession") pushed this campaign right over the top…

To Anne, whose art inspired me to move forward with my illustrations and whose work I am happy to say graces this book...

And to C. L. Jarvis, for her consistent support of my works.

My deepest and most heartfelt thanks!

To my friends and family all of whom support me in so many ways, from telling me I am amazing when I question myself to picking up dinner when I am in the weeds.

I love you all.

And last but never least, to my grandmama, Gertrude Vonderau, who if she were still around would be hitting me with her whisk broom for putting her name down on paper. Thank you for my love of gardening and cooking and for the big red books that started this all. But most of all, thank you for giving me a place to dream.

The Seven Sisters' Fairytales

Table of Contents

A Gray Day

ODne day when the sky outside had turned to gray and the gathering clouds promised that rain was sure to come, seven sisters sat down and took up their weaving, as they always did on such days.

"Let us tell some tales to pass the time away," said the Violet sister as she drew a thread through her fingers.

"We can share tales of love," said the Blue sister.

"And of loyalty," said the Green sister.

"Tales of quests..." said the Yellow sister.

"And curses..." said the Orange sister

"And determination," finished the Indigo sister.

"Well, I have a tale that may have a little of all of those," said the Red sister, and she began the weaving with a thread in a bold color as suited her.

The Red Sister's Tale

The Swan Maiden

I have heard tell that there once grew the most beautiful pear tree. It stood in the very center of a castle garden, surrounded by high walls, and from its branches hung exactly twenty-four perfect golden pears.

The king, whose garden it was, adored this pear tree and took great delight in going out every morning to count the twenty-four golden pears that grew from it. But one morning when he went to visit his beloved pear tree, he found only twenty-three golden pears hanging from its branches.

He spent the rest of his day questioning everyone in the castle, from the youngest scullery maid to the captain of the guard, but no one knew anything about the missing pear. The very next morning it happened again, despite the extra guards that had been set to watch over it the night before.

Frustrated, the king called his three sons to him and set them a challenge. Whoever could catch the thief would be given half the kingdom and inherit the rest after the king's death. The three princes talked amongst themselves, and it was decided that it would only be fair that the eldest be the first to try.

So that night the eldest prince sat beneath the pear tree, gun in hand, and waited for the thief to show themselves. But when the morning came, another golden pear was missing, and no thief had been seen.

The prince found that he could not say what had happened. He swore that he did not remember closing his eyes, even for a moment, and had been as surprised as anyone to wake with the morning sun on his face. Embarrassed, he urged the second prince to take his turn the following evening. But the second prince had no better luck than the first. Bewildered, they ceded the next night to the youngest prince so that he might have his chance.

Now all three princes were handsome, brave and true, but the youngest was perhaps just a little cleverer than his brothers. While the first two princes had kept their vigils, he had talked with the palace guards whom the king had first set to watch the pear tree. Most did not remember any more than the princes had, but one old soldier recalled hearing the most beautiful music for just a moment before waking up with the cock crowing a welcome to the silvery dawn.

The story made the youngest prince wonder. So, when evening came and it was his turn to watch for the pear thief, he had a plan.

He sat at the base of the tree with his gun across his knees, just as his brothers had done the nights before. But keeping in mind what the old guard had said, he used softened wax to stop up his ears, which meant he was as deaf as a post as he kept his vigil.

That is why when midnight came and the unearthly music began to play, the prince heard none of it. So, he was wide awake when a couple of hours later the branches above him began to shake. He saw among the leaves an enormous swan reaching with its beak for one of the golden pears. Slowly he raised his gun and took aim, only to find a breath-takingly beautiful woman in his sights where once the swan had been. He could see her lips moving as she pleaded at him with her eyes.

Lowering his gun, he removed the wax from his ears so that he could hear what it was she was saying.

"Don't shoot, king's son." Her lilting voice, as sweet as birdsong, trembled slightly.

"I will not," the prince promised. "Though I will admit, lady thief, it is mostly for the chance to know you better."

"I am not a thief by choice," confessed the Swan Maiden. "My mistress is the witch with three eyes, and it is she who sends me out every night to bring her back a golden pear from the king's tree. And if you want to woo me, then it is she that you will have to free me from."

"Then so I shall," said the prince, already quite enamored with the lovely woman sitting in the branches above him.

"She lives far from here. Over seven high mountains, and across seven deep valleys with seven wide rivers running through them. Are you bold to go that far?" she asked.

"Yes," he declared confidently. "I am bold enough, for that and much more."

"And are you clever enough, I wonder?"

"I am," he said assuredly.

"We will see," she said. Jumping lightly from the branch, she landed gracefully in front of him and became a swan once more. "Climb onto my back, king's son, and hold on tight."

Once he had done as she bade him, the great swan spread her wings and sprang into the air.

Through the night sky they flew, the stars a blanket above them. Below them rose seven high mountains, which fell into seven deep valleys with seven wide rivers winding through them like silver ribbons. On and on they flew until he saw in the distance a dark hill crowned by a house that shone like fire.

"Yonder hut is where the witch with three eyes lives," said the Swan Maiden. "If you are bold enough, knock on her door and when she asks what you have come for, tell her you have come for the one who draws the water and builds the fire, for that is myself."

With that, the great swan landed on the top of the hill. The prince slid from her back, and she flew off again, over the top of the roof.

The prince stepped boldly up to the door, as he had said he would, and knocked with a rap! tap! tap! The witch herself opened it.

"And what do you want?" she asked.

"I have come for the one who draws the water and builds the fire," he answered.

The old witch scowled at him, which with her three eyes was a frightful sight indeed.

"Very well. You can have what you came for if you can clean my stables tomorrow between the rising and setting of the sun. But you should know, if you fail in the doing, then you will be torn to pieces, body and bone," she warned him and shut the door in his face.

But the prince was not to be scared away by empty words. Stretching out along the ground, he waited for the sun to rise.

The next morning the witch came and led him to the stables where he was to do his task. The stable was huge, in it were at least a hundred cattle, and it looked as if it had been ten years since anyone had last cleaned it.

"Here you are," said the witch handing him a pitchfork and broom, cackling all the while. Then she left him.

The prince did not hesitate despite the impossible task, instead he set to his work with a will. But he might as well have tried to bail out the ocean with a pail, because though he worked harder than any ten men could have, by the time the sun was high in the sky, he had made almost no headway.

At noon he was surprised to see the lovely Swan Maiden standing at the stable doors, beckoning to him. Leaving his pitchfork and broom, he went to join her.

"When one is tired, one should rest," she said taking his hand in hers.

She led him to a sunny spot just outside the stable. There she sat and bade the prince to join her and lay his head in her lap.

So, he did, happy to take her advice. After all, he had gained nothing from working so hard at his task, and perhaps if he were to take a moment, a clever solution would come to him.

The prince lay with his head quietly in the Swan Maiden's lap, watching cloud ships sail across the sky, while she combed his hair with a golden comb. He was thinking so hard of a way to complete his task that he did not even realize that he had fallen fast asleep.

When he woke, the Swan Maiden was gone and to his horror he found the sun was near to setting. He jumped up and went to the stable, only to find it clean as a plate.

He had barely recovered from his shock, when he heard the old witch's footsteps coming up the path. Swiftly he set about, clearing away a straw here and a speck there, as if he were just finishing his work.

"You never did this by yourself!" exclaimed the witch, her face as dark as a thunderstorm.

"That may be so, and it may not be so," said the king's son. "But you lent no hand to help. So, now may I have the one who draws the water and builds the fire?"

"No," said the witch shaking her head. "There is more yet to be done before you can have what you asked for. Tomorrow, if you can thatch the roof of this stable with bird feathers, no two being the same color, and do it between the rising and setting of the sun, then you can have your sweetheart and welcome. But if you fail, I will grind your bones finer than malt in a mill."

That suited the prince well enough. So, at sunrise, he took his gun and went into the fields. But if there were any birds to shoot, he did not see them.

By the time the sun was high in the sky, he had only two feathers and those were of the same color.

At noon, the Swan Maiden came to see him as she had the day before.

"One should not tramp and tramp all day without any rest," she said.

Taking his hand in hers, she led him to a spot where the grass was soft and sweet smelling. There they sat and he laid his head in her lap where she once again combed his hair with a golden comb until he was fast asleep.

He opened his eyes to see that the sun was setting, and his work was done just as it had been before. When he heard the old witch coming, he hopped up onto the stable roof and began to shift things here and there, for all the world as though he were just finishing his work.

"You never did that work alone!" exclaimed the witch when she saw the stable roof with its thatch of feathers.

"That may be so, and it may not be so," said the king's son. "But all the same it was none of your doing. So, now may I have the one who draws the water and builds the fire?"

But the witch shook her head. "No," she said, "there is still another task for you to do. Over yonder there is a fir tree. At the very top of this tree is a crow's nest with three eggs in it. If you can reach the nest and bring back all three eggs without losing or breaking a single one and do it between the rising and the setting of the sun tomorrow, then you may have that which you have asked me for."

That suited the prince just fine. So, the next morning he woke with the sun and headed off to find the fir tree.

Finding it was not hard for it was more than a hundred feet high. Climbing it proved much harder. Ten men standing on each other's shoulders could not reach the bottom branches, and the trunk itself was as smooth as glass from root to tip. Despite that, the prince tried his best to scale the fir tree and for all his trouble he could only make it up a few feet before sliding right back down. He could well have tried to climb a moonbeam.

By and by, the Swan Maiden came as she had done before.

"Are trying to climb the fir tree?" she asked.

"Indeed," replied the prince.

"And how are you fairing?"

"None too well," the prince admitted, sheepishly.

The Swan Maiden smiled at him. "Then perhaps I can help you," she said.

She unbound her braids until her golden hair hung down all about and lay piled high on the ground around her. Then she began to sing. She sang and she sang until the wind began to blow. Catching up the maiden's hair, it carried it up to the top of the fir tree and once there tied it to the upper most branches.

Quickly the prince climbed up the shining strands until he reached the very top. There was the nest with three eggs in it, just as the witch had said. He gathered them up and carefully went back down the same way that he had come up.

Once he was back on the ground, the wind came again to loosen the maiden's hair from the fir tree's branches and carried it back to her. She bound it up just as it was before.

"Now listen," said the Swan Maiden, "when the witch asks you for the crow's eggs that you have gathered, tell her that they belong to the one who gathered them. Do not worry, she cannot take them from you, and they are worth something, I promise you."

At sunset the old witch came hobbling along to where the prince sat at the foot of the fir tree.

"Have you gathered the crow's eggs?" she asked.

"Yes," replied the prince. "They are here in my handkerchief. And now may I have the one who draws the water and builds the fire?"

"Yes," said the witch, "you may have her, only give me my crow's eggs."

"No," he said firmly. "The crow's eggs are none of yours. They belong to the one who gathered them."

Realizing that she would not get them that way, the witch tried another.

"Come, come now," said the witch in tones as sweet as honey. "There should be no hard feelings between us! Before heading home with what you came for, you should have a good supper. After all, you have served me faithfully, and it is ill to travel on an empty stomach."

So, she led the prince back to the house. There she sat him down and went to put the pot on to boil and sharpen the bread knife on the stone stoop.

While the prince was waiting for the witch, there came a tap at the door, and who should it be but the Swan Maiden.

"Come with me," she said, "and mind that you bring the crow's eggs. The knife she is sharpening is for you, and so is the pot on the fire. She means to cook you up this very night and pick your bones in the morning."

The prince followed the Swan Maiden down to the kitchen, and there they fashioned a figure made up of barley meal and honey.

The Swan Maiden dressed the figure in her own clothes, and together they placed it on a stool in the chimney corner. There it sat, soft and sticky, but looking much like the Swan Maiden in the fire's soft light.

She led the prince from the kitchen and through the front door, which was opposite the one where the witch sat sharpening her knife. Once they were out under the evening sky, she became a swan again and taking the prince on her back, she flew away.

Not long after they had gone, the witch came in from sharpening her knife to find that the prince was nowhere to be seen. Try as she might, she could find no trace of him. In a rage, she stormed through the house until she came to the kitchen and saw the figure that was sitting there.

"Where is your sweetheart," the witch asked the barley woman, thinking it the maiden herself, but of course the barley woman did not answer.

"Answer me you ungrateful creature!" she cried. "Or do you hope to protect him by staying dumb?" Raising her hand, she slapped the barley woman as hard as she could. - Thwack! - Her hand stuck fast in the honey and barley meal.

10

"What! You insolent creature! Let go of me!"

Thwack! - she struck the barley woman hard with her other hand which also sank in deep.

So, there she stood, unable to get herself unstuck from the honey and barley meal, and could still be there to this day, for all we know.

As for the Swan Maiden and the prince, they flew back over the seven high mountains with their seven deep valleys and the seven wide rivers winding through them. They flew on and on until they came near the prince's own kingdom. There the Swan Maiden landed in a great wide field that lay only a few miles from the king's castle. She bade the prince take out the first crow's egg and open it.

He did as she suggested, and what should he find inside but the most beautiful little castle, made all of gold and silver. He set the palace on the ground, and it grew and grew until it covered a whole acre of land.

Then she bade him to break open the second egg, and out came great herds of cattle and sheep, enough to cover the meadow where they stood.

Finally, she told him to break open the third egg, and from it came scores of servants all dressed in gold and silver livery.

That morning when the king woke and looked out his bedroom window, he found just on the horizon a splendid castle of gold and silver shining in the morning light. Astonished, he gathered his people together and rode over to see how such a thing had come to be.

On the way, they rode through herds of cattle and sheep, fat and content where they grazed. And past rows of servants, dressed all in gold and silver, happily going about their labor. On and on they rode until they came to the castle gate, where the prince waited.

Upon their arrival, the prince greeted his father and told him all of what had happened. The king listened intently, relieved at having his son returned safe (and overjoyed knowing his pears would now be safe as well). Only the two elder princes seemed uncertain, thinking that the youngest of them, having found the pear thief, was to inherit the whole of the kingdom. But their minds were soon put to rest. The youngest prince insisted that he had more than enough of his own and saw no need to have his father's kingdom as well.

Soon he and the Swan Maiden were married, and a grand wedding it was. The guests made very merry and danced the whole night long. As the night grew older and the wedding guests began to depart, the prince sat happily with his new wife and watched them all go.

"Despite what I had promised you when first we met, I can't say that I did much that was very bold or very clever, save to follow your advice when you gave it," the prince admitted to his new wife.

She smiled brightly at her husband. "Some may say that is true, and some may say it's not. As for me, I would say there is no cleverer thing than to follow good advice."

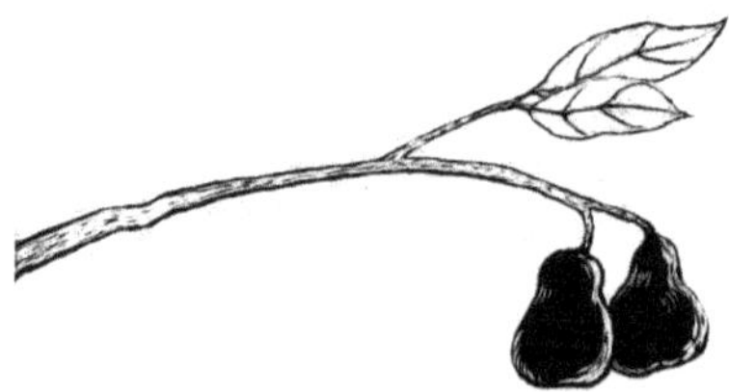

The sisters laughed at hearing the end of the tale, and all agreed that sometimes the cleverest thing one can do is to follow another's advice.

"Who else has a tale to tell?" The Violet sister asked.

"I have one," the Orange sister said as she added her thread to the weaving. "It is a tale of secrets and curses and love that blooms unexpectedly.

The Orange Sisters' Tale

The Tiger Prince

There were once two young women, one as different from the other as the sun is from the moon.

The first young woman, Naomi, was the daughter of a great sea captain. She had traveled the world 'round on her father's ship, from the icy fjords in the north to the dune edged seas in the south and was well known for being bold and fearless.

The other, Oriane, was the daughter of a prosperous merchant family. She was sweet natured and possessed a generous heart but was also shy and terribly timid.

Even in looks, they were quite different. Naomi's hair was dark and wild, her skin kissed golden by the sun. Oriane's skin was the palest cream, and her heavy gold hair hung in a sleek braid to her knees. They were opposite in nearly every way, save for their eyes. Both had clear, blue-gray eyes.

So, it came to be that Oriane, while journeying towards a distant land, found herself aboard the very same ship Naomi's father captained. The two young women quickly became fast friends, much to everyone's amazement. And by the end of the voyage, they were closer than even two sisters could be.

One night, just before they were about to put into port, they sat in Naomi's cabin, as they often did in the evening. But on this night, unlike all the others, Oriane seemed to have something heavy weighing on her thoughts. Concerned, Naomi asked what it was that was troubling her.

With a great sigh, the merchant's daughter confided in her friend, confessing that her family was no longer as prosperous as they once had been. In fact, their fortune was all but gone, and she had set out on this journey with what was the last of her family's money in the hopes of helping improve their situation.

She told Naomi about stories that had reached her homeland. Stories of a bespelled prince that promised numerous riches to whomever could unravel the mysteries of his curse. So Oraine's father, desperate to avoid ruin, had sent a letter to the king of that distant land, the very land towards which they now sailed, in the hopes that his daughter might succeed where others had failed. And in doing so, save her family from destitution.

Now Naomi could see her friend's determination to do what she could to help her family. But she could also hear the tremor in her friend's voice and feel the shaking in her hands.

"Have no fear, sister of my heart. I will come with you, and between the two of us we are sure to best any curse!" she assured her.

That very night, Naomi went to her father, the sea captain, and told him of her plans to accompany her friend. Her father agreed, having learned long ago that his daughter was quite capable and certainly able to make up her own mind. In fact, he thought the whole adventure might be good for her. So, the next day, when they put into dock, he saw them off with some practical advice and well wishes.

Arm in arm, the two young women left the ship. Waiting for them on the docks was a lovely carriage drawn by four horses as white as moonflowers. A footman helped them up into it and they proceeded to ride down beautifully paved streets, past busy markets filled with wondrous sights and delicious smells. Laughing children raced next to the carriage, waving at them as they drove past.

Eventually they arrived at a palace that sat glowing like a pearl on the edge of a vast lake. They made their way up its broad steps to where the great front doors stood open invitingly. There they were met by a kindly steward who led them inside. They followed him through arch-lined courtyards, big and small, where fountains tiled in brilliant colors filled the air with the soft music of falling water. They soon came to a garden terrace that overlooked the shining lake. And there they met the king, who invited them to sit with him and ordered that tea be brought.

The king was hail and handsome, and spoke kindly to them as they sat eating delicate little cakes and drinking spiced apple tea. He smiled often as he fed the tiny golden bird who sat quite boldly on his shoulder. Still, for all his graciousness, there was a cloak of sadness that hung over him, which added a gauntness to his cheeks and shadows to his eyes.

They talked all through the afternoon, with the king asking about Oriane's journey and the many adventures of Naomi's childhood. In fact, they talked of everything except the prince for whom they had come, until the sky began to darken into twilight. As the shadows of dusk deepened across the vast lake, an island appeared from nowhere. It seemed to take shape from the very air itself, much to the amazement of the two young women. On its shore was a palace, with elegant glass-domed rooftops and walls lined with graceful arches.

It was then that the king told them of his son, the prince, who had been spirited away as a babe and taken to the very island that they saw before them. And to the king's knowledge, he had been there ever since.

Awed by this revelation, the young women bubbled with questions. Had anyone tried to sail to the island? Had they tried to build a bridge? How was the king sure that his son was still there? (Neither young woman could bring themselves to ask how the king knew his son was still alive).

He told them of how the bridges that they had tried to build had met with disaster. And how every boat that had tried to sail the lake's waters had been plagued with ill luck so that they had had to turn back. Most had sunk. But when it came to the question of knowing whether the prince was still on the island, the king's eyes saddened further. The little golden bird who was still perched on his shoulder rubbed its head against his cheek seemingly in sympathy. Oriane too, reached out to comfort the king.

"You have not seen or spoken to your son in all these years?" she asked.

"I have seen him only through the lens of a spyglass," admitted the king. "For a few hours, every day at dawn and at dusk when the island appears. And I have spoken to him, after a fashion, through letters delivered to the palace."

"Delivered by whom?" Naomi asked boldly.

"A very curious messenger whom I do not question. But if I were to tell you who it was, then surely you would doubt my sanity."

The king, knowing the reason they had come, had already ordered a suite of rooms prepared for them in the palace. Which is where they were led to shortly after the king had finished answering their questions. The rooms were spacious and lovely with two bedrooms, a sitting room and a wide door which opened out onto a balcony overlooking the lake.

The next morning and everyday there after, they sat on that same balcony for breakfast, beneath an arbor draped in wisteria. They would sip warm chocolate tea and eat buttery pastries while they watched giant water lilies rise up from the lake. The young women marveled as lily pads the size of small boats unfurled themselves over the water's surface. Their flowers stood like a forest of small trees, their pale pink petals opening wide in the morning sun. Gigantic fish slept in the water lilies' shade; their golden scales glittering and flashing deep below the surface of the tea-colored water. It was no small wonder why boats did not venture out onto the lake; few would survive a single swish from those mighty tails.

When the sun reached midday, the water lilies would fold in their petals and the lily pads would curl themselves back up. The fish would awaken, their giant golden bodies making the water eddy and swirl. The island itself would be lost, disappearing in the dazzling light off the water. Not to be seen again until that evening when it would reappear in the dusk's silvery shade, bringing with it a truly wondrous and terrifying sight.

It strode down the street below their balcony, with a coat like fire, a prince among tigers. He stood nearly as tall as a horse, yet to their utter amazement, none of the people on the street seemed to be afraid as he passed them by.

Oriane nearly fainted with fear at the sight of him. But Naomi watched in wonder as the great beast stepped up to the edge of the water, and gathering his haunches beneath him, leapt easily across the whole of the lake.

For days, the young women watched the island appear and disappear with nary a clue as to how to reach it. On the seventh morning, they were just sitting down to breakfast beneath the wisteria when the little golden bird (whom they had first seen sitting on the king's shoulder) came to join them. It sang and chirped in the most soothing manner while the young women fed it crumbs from their plates and pondered, without much success, upon how Oriane could reach the island.

Then, Naomi noticed the little bird did the most curious thing. She watched as it plucked several leaves from the wisteria that was close by, placing them in a row along the stone balustrade. It chirped and hopped from one leaf to another, and back again. Its peculiar antics gave her an idea.

Turning to her friend she said, "You know, those lily pads remind me a bit of floating docks, like the ones at the port where you came aboard my father's ship. Do you remember? You came across those handily enough, and I believe you could cross over the lily pads just as easily. In fact, I am sure of it!"

Oriane did not agree with her friend. She remembered how terrified she was to step out onto those docks. How they shifted and bobbed beneath her feet. But she was determined to do what she could to change her family's fortune.

"I can but try," she said.

So, they quickly dressed her in a flowing silver dress, over top which they added a sapphire coat. They put pearl slippers on her feet and a jeweled clasp at her waist. Naomi braided her friend's long golden hair before covering it all with a hat and veil. The veil fell to the young woman's breast, obscuring her face and her hair, as was the custom of her people when a young woman went unchaperoned to meet a potential suitor.

Together the two young women went down to the lake shore. Oriane took a deep breath and gingerly stepped out onto the closest lily pad. When it stayed steady under her foot, she took another step.

Confidence bloomed in Oriane's heart. She smiled back at Naomi, then with feet as light as butterflies, she continued along the water lily road to the prince's island.

Naomi kept vigil for the rest of the morning. At midday, just before the lily pads were about to begin curling up for the day, she saw her friend returning.

Even from far away, Oriane's happiness was unmistakable, her feet almost danced down the leafy path towards the shore where Naomi waited.

"It was wonderful!" she exclaimed, her smile radiant, as she leapt lightly to the shore and hugged Naomi.

Arm in arm, the two young women walked back to the palace where they sat beneath the wisteria for the rest of the afternoon as Oriane told Naomi of her meeting with the prince. In fact, she could not stop talking about him! For it seemed that, at least in Oriane's eyes, he was all the things a prince should be.

But as the afternoon waned so did her happiness. The curse had not allowed the prince to tell her more than she already knew. However, he could tell her that she would have to come to him every morning and return each evening if she was to have any hope of unraveling the curse.

Needless to say, as the time for her to return came closer, Oriane's worry grew. Hadn't they already mulled over this whole week past all the ways she could possibly cross to the island? It was only just this morning that they had considered the water lily road, a road that was not there now. She could not stop the sense of despair growing in her chest.

Naomi hated to see the unhappiness in her friend's eyes. Yet, no new ideas of how to return to the island that evening came to mind, no matter which way she looked at their dilemma. Even she began to feel a little desperate as the dying sun's light grew thicker, covering the land in golden honey.

Then, in the distance, Naomi saw the tiger walking down the road towards them, a living flame made flesh. Children were running up to him as they sometimes did, laughing as they made a great game out of seeing who could touch his tail before he flicked it away.

Suddenly, she had a bold idea.

"My dearest friend, I think I know how you could return to the island, but you would have to be very brave," she said excitedly. "Every evening at dusk, the tiger walks beneath our balcony before he makes his leap to the island. I am sure that if you were to jump on his back, he could carry you with him."

Oriane looked at Naomi horrified, her heart quailing at the idea. She tried to steel herself, but tears filled her eyes. She gripped her hands tightly and trembled.

"I want to!" she cried. "I want to be brave, and I did my best crossing the lily pads this morning. But I am not like you, sister of my heart. It may have seemed like a small task to you, but it took all my nerve, and I have no more." The tears were now chasing themselves down her cheeks in silvery rivers. She looked as if her tender heart was crumbling to pieces.

Naomi had no wish to see her friend so heartbroken, and she wanted her to succeed in her quest to help her family. Another idea flashed into her mind like a lightning bolt. She took Oriane by the hand and led her hastily to their rooms.

"There may still be a way," she said. "Quick, give me your gown, slippers and veil. I will ride on the back of tiger for you! Then when I return, I can tell you all that I find."

Concern and hope warred in Oriane's face as she quickly stripped out of her gown and helped Naomi into it.

"But, how will you get back," she asked, fearing for her friend. She would rather her family's entire fortune lost than lose this woman she held so dear.

But Naomi laughed, for this was just the kind of adventure she loved.

"Have no fear!" she said as she put on the pearl slippers and pulled the veil over her dark hair. "I am sure I will find a way. And don't worry, we will rescue your prince!" She waved and rushed out onto the balcony as Oriane watched from behind the bedroom door.

Naomi hoped that the tiger had not already passed them by. But as luck would have it, the great tiger was on the street just below.

She already had one slippered foot on the balustrade when she called out fearlessly, "Pardon me, master tiger, but I need your help!" And with that, she leapt from the railing, her gown and veil fluttering behind her like sapphire wings. She landed lightly on his back.

The great cat stopped and looked over his shoulder at her with golden-green eyes. She realized just how *large* the tiger was. And for the first time in her life, Naomi wondered if perhaps she had been a little too bold.

"Please," she said contritely, "It is very important that I go to the prince's island. Would you carry me with you?"

The tiger nodded his head, before continuing on. Naomi felt as though she was back on a ship in rough seas because although she might, with luck and skill,

be able to ride such a powerful creature, she surely could not control him.

He brought them to the water's edge. Naomi felt the strong muscles gather beneath her, then suddenly, like tightly held springs let lose, the tiger leapt, carrying her out over the dark lake. On and on they went, as though they flew on the back of the evening wind, until they landed on the opposite shore.

The tiger did not stop but continued to

carry her to a small courtyard where night-blooming jasmine grew, and moonflowers hung in curtains on the stone walls. It was there that they were met by the prince.

He was every bit as handsome as Oriane had described, with hair the color of midnight and curious eyes; one of which was the palest gold and the other as green as clear jade. Both were filled with kindness.

He offered his hand to Naomi as she slid from the tiger's back and led her to a room lined with tall arched windows that overlooked the lake. At its center was a table, where he offered her a seat most courteously. He then went over to a large cupboard, and opening it, took out gold-edged dishes filled with dainty rolls and sugared fruits which he placed on the table in front of her.

Once all the dishes were on the table, he sat across from her and they ate. All the foods offered had been conscientiously prepared so that she would not have to remove her veil to eat. It showed a thoughtfulness that in Naomi's experience was uncommon. And she thought that this prince would be a perfect match for her friend, should they decide to wed.

However, Naomi was surprised at how shy the prince seemed. From the tales Oriane had told, she had expected someone of a bolder nature. But perhaps he had seemed bold to someone of her friend's gentler ways.

By the time they had finished eating, it was obvious to Naomi that the prince was well read and possessed an inquisitive mind. He asked her questions about the world beyond the island as they strolled through the gardens with their glass-domed ceilings; and shared with her all the things he had learned from the books he had read and his study of the stars.

She, in turn, told him of the wondrous sights she had seen and the strange skies she traveled under. In fact, she was enjoying the conversation so much that she had forgotten that she was supposed to be Oriane, and not herself. But if the prince had noticed any difference, he was too polite to say.

They talked until just before midnight, then returned to the courtyard where she had first arrived. There, he bid her goodnight, promising that the tiger would arrive soon to carry her back across the lake.

As promised, the tiger appeared moments after the prince had left. He carried her back across the lake, and right up into the palace itself. There they parted company. Naomi watched as the tiger headed deeper into the palace, and then suddenly she knew just who it was that brought the king his letters.

When Naomi returned to their rooms, she found Oriane waiting up for her. She shared with her friend all that had happened and everything that was said during her visit with the prince. They talked the night away, sleeping only a few hours before the morning sun lifted its shining head into the sky.

They ate breakfast quickly, then headed down to the shore as soon as they were finished to wait for the water lilies to unfurled their leafy road.

So, the season passed in much the same way. Nearly everyday after Oriane had returned from visiting the prince, she would sit with the king to share his midday meal. She would tell him of his son, and he in turn, would tell her stories of himself, so that she might share them with the prince.

This was how they learned about the queen and her sister. Both had been powerful enchantresses whom the king had met in his travels. The king had fallen in love with the eldest, but when he and his would-be queen announced their decision to marry, the younger sister flew into a rage. It seemed that she too had fallen in love with the king, unbeknownst to him. She cursed their union bitterly, and soon became so consumed by jealousy that it turned her into a twisted, ugly thing; a fearsome hag who believed herself betrayed by her sister.

But Oriane was not the only one to learn something interesting. While she was away visiting with the cursed prince, Naomi became good friends with many of the servants, who believed her to be the handmaiden of the merchant's golden-haired daughter. That was how she came to be so often in the kitchen, which was where she learned what had happened on the fateful day when the prince was taken.

According to the cook, who was an authority on such matters, on the very morning of the prince's birth a fearsome tigress had come right up into the palace and taken the baby away.

The butler, who was listening as he polished the silver, insisted that she remembered wrong. He was there that evening when the tigress had walked boldly up into the palace and stolen away the new born prince.

They argued over this often, however, both agreed that the prince had not set foot on the mainland since, and that it was from that day on that the island had begun to vanish and the lake had become a place where ships dare not sail. It was at that same time that the queen disappeared, leaving the king to mourn both his wife and his son.

But as interesting as all that was, it was not all Naomi learned while sitting in the kitchen. She also learned of the magic cupboard.

One day, upon her return, Oriane told Naomi of the most delightful cake that she had eaten while visiting with the prince. It was light and fluffy, covered with delicate cream frosting and fresh strawberries.

Naomi remembered the cook placing just such a cake in a great wooden cupboard in the kitchen. However, she never remembered anyone removing it. Which begged the question, how did the prince get his food? Curious, Naomi proposed a test to see if it had truly been the same cake.

The next morning Naomi went down to the kitchen, as she usually did when Oriane visited the island. She watched as food was put into the cupboard. And when the cook stepped away for a moment, leaving its door open, Naomi quickly placed a small spray of wisteria next to one of the cakes. She turned the plate so that it would not be easily seen. Then she waited.

The cook returned, closing the door firmly after she had added a warm pot of apple tea.

Even though Naomi stayed in the kitchen far longer than was her custom, she saw no one come to take away the food that had been placed in the cupboard. In fact, no one opened the cupboard at all.

At noon she returned to their rooms. Oriane arrived soon after, the spray of wisteria tucked in her jeweled belt.

They talked for the rest of the day as was their habit. Oriane confirmed that the spray of wisteria had been beside the cake which had come from the cupboard. She also showed Naomi another flower, a beautiful orchid, which she said the prince had given to her. She happily recounted the tale of how he had scaled the rocks near a waterfall they often visited (the island being much larger than it looked from the shore) just so that he could give it to her. She went on to praise his fearless nature and adventurous spirit.

This made Naomi think back to her own conversations with the prince. They had been interesting and varied. And she had often thought that the prince would make a wonderful husband for the sister of her heart (and though she might not admit it, for herself as well). However, she never would have described him as having an adventurous spirit. Nor could she see him giving her a flower such as the one he had given Oriane. She felt sure that the flower he would have given her would more likely be something like meadowsweet or marsh mallow. A flower whose beauty was subtle and its virtue deeper.

"You know, sister mine, if I did not know better, I would say that we were speaking about two different men." Naomi ruminated. "The prince whom I have spent these many evenings with is interesting and deeply read. He has a thirst for knowledge and is captivated by the tales of my travels. However, I would not say that he has an adventurous spirit. Nor would I call him bold, but rather I would tend to think him reserved. Tell me again, is your prince tall, with night-dark hair and a generous mouth?" she asked her friend.

"Yes," said Oriane, "and his left eye is as bright as a gold coin, while his right is a clear jade green."

"Huh, curious," Naomi said, "because I would have sworn that it was his right eye that was gold and his left green."

"Could that be a clue to the curse?" Oriane wondered.

"Perhaps," Naomi agreed. "If we could but both see him at the same time, I think all would be made clear. After all, it is not by a person's look that you truly know them."

So, the two friends devised a plan, and that very evening they set it into motion. Naomi left to meet the prince as she usually did, riding on the tiger's back as he flew across the lake.

Meanwhile, Oriane, cloaked and veiled, carefully hid herself. When she thought that all the servants were elsewhere, she followed the instructions given to her by Naomi and crept down to the kitchen. Heart pounding with fear, she opened the cupboard to find it empty. Carefully, she folded herself up inside, then steeling her nerve, closed the door and waited for she knew not what.

As soon as the door clicked shut, she heard voices. It was not the cook or one of the other servants, but her friend's well-loved voice and another that she had just recently come to also hold dear... No, that was not quite right. The pitch and timber were the same, but the manner of speech was not.

Carefully, she cracked open the cupboard door. The room she looked out onto was familiar with its tall arched windows looking out over the moon-silvered lake. And there before her was her dearest friend talking with the prince. It was in that moment, Oriane realized that her friend had also fallen in love.

Anxious butterflies fluttered in her stomach, as she listened to the sister of her heart talk with the prince that she, herself, had come to love as well.

But the longer Oriane listened, the more the butterflies settled. There was no doubt that this was not the bold prince she knew. And when she heard Naomi begin to speak of the curse, she quietly slipped out of the cupboard.

"My prince," Naomi said, as they stood watching the moon on the water. "I think I can solve the riddle of your curse. If I am right, then this land has not one, but two princes. I believe your mother, being a powerful enchantress, changed her shape. She was the tigress that carried first your brother and then you across to this island. And I believe she did it all because she was afraid of what her sister's curse might call down upon your heads."

"Right in one, you clever, clever woman!" He said as he picked her up and spun her around, the prince's smile bright as the morning sun as he looked up at her.

"Yes, well done," said a voice that both musical and light.

The prince set Naomi's feet back down on the ground, but kept her hand clasped firmly in his own. They both turned to find the little golden bird perched on a settee.

"Do you know me?" The little bird asked.

"Yes, your majesty," Naomi replied, having guessed that it could only be the lost queen to whom she was speaking.

The golden bird nodded her dainty head in acknowledgment.

"You have indeed solved the curse's riddle and as such are entitled to the fortune promised you. But, if there is more that you seek, and by the way that you hold my son's hand I must guess there is, then the curse still has to be broken." A look of pity washed over the queen's face. "Though I wonder what the sister of your heart, as you, yourself, have called her, would say if she were to see you holding my son's hand thus."

"I would wish her well, with all my heart," said Oriane, stepping out from beside the cupboard; where up till then, she had been watching as things unfolded. "Even if she were holding the hand of the man I love, but thankfully she is not."

Without hesitation Oriane crossed the courtyard to where the great tiger waited in the shadows. There was not the slightest tremor in her hands as she bravely placed them on either side of his fierce head and looked up into his eyes.

"The one I love is here," she said.

"Are you sure, child?" the queen asked.

"I am," said Oriane. "For it is his heart I know, not the shape he wears."

And with that, where once stood a tiger now stood a man. Truly, he did have the same look as the prince who stood next to Naomi. Though seeing them together, it could be said that Naomi's prince, the younger of the two (if only by a few minutes), stood just a little taller than Oriane's. Though her prince, the elder, had just a touch more breadth in his shoulders.

The elder prince picked Oriane up and spun her around, much as his brother had just done to Naomi, smiling up at her all the while.

"Brave and beautiful! For all your protestations, I knew you had a strength within that you did not see," said the elder prince.

"How can you say 'beautiful' when you have seen neither of us unveiled?" Oriane asked shyly, for it was true that both she and Naomi were still veiled.

"Just as you knew my brother," said the younger prince turning to Naomi. "With our hearts. For it was not your looks we fell in love with." At that, both young women lifted their veils, each smiling up at their prince.

Soon after, both princes changed back into tigers, for they were their mother's sons, and now that the curse no longer bound them, they could change at will. With both Oriane and Naomi on their backs, they leapt across the lake with the little golden bird following close behind them. They went straight to the palace. And when they all stood before the king, the queen, still in her guise of a little bird, asked him to name who she was. He did. There was a shower of golden feathers which revealed a lovely woman with hair was as dark as the princes though both her eyes were a bright and shining gold.

The queen had been worried that the king would be angry at her, for all that he had had to endure. She need not have feared, for when the king saw his lost wife before him, their sons at her side, there was no room for anger in his heart, nor sadness either. All of that fell away as soon as he eyes rested upon them.

He hugged his wife, and like his sons, lifted her from her feet to spin her around in his joy, and the elegant queen laughed and laughed.

It was not long after that the two young women, Naomi and Oriane, became sisters in truth, marrying the princes they loved.

Her family's fortune saved, Oriane and the eldest prince stayed at the palace with the king and queen, for although she had found that she was indeed fearless, she still preferred her adventures to be small.

Naomi and the younger prince, however, chose to return to her father's ship where they went to see all the places that the prince had only ever read about. But they visited often to share their tales with those they held most dear.

And what about the queen's sister, one might ask. The sister whose jealousy had twisted her so much that the queen feared for her sons? The very one whose curse led to all the events about which this tale was told?

Well, it is said that someone found her heart and she herself got the ending she deserved... but that is another tale entirely.

"Which goes to show that even curses are not always what they seem," the Orange sister finished

"It is true," The Yellow sister agreed, nodding knowingly as she added her own thread to the weave. "I too have heard a tale where one thing was sometimes another. And where a curse may not have been a curse at all, but rather a blessing in disguise."

The Yellow Sister's Tale

The Fish Who Was Sometimes A Boy *or* The Golden Fish Scale

Long, long ago, there was a very poor town on the edge of a wide dreary river. The town had not always been poor, and the river along which it sat had not always been so dreary. In fact, once it had been said to be the most beautiful river under heaven.

In this town lived a young girl named Nobuko. She lived there with her mother, father, and grandmother. They were also extremely poor, just like the rest of the town, but it hadn't always been that way. Seven years before, when Nobuko had been only a year old, the river had begun to turn dirty and foul. With the change in the river came a change in the town's fortunes, and in the fortunes of Nobuko's family as well.

Still, Nobuko thought herself lucky because she had been able to find respectable work in the household of a young widow of high esteem.

The young widow's house was on the other side of the river where the oldest and most influential families lived. Every morning, Nobuko traveled over the long wooden bridges to the young widow's house. There she would clean out the ashes and scrub the floors; sweep the walks and beat the rugs; and anything else the head housekeeper told her to do.

The head housekeeper was a tall woman, with odd yellow eyes and a wide mouth. She ran a strict household, and the few servants that still worked there lived in fear of angering her. Though to be fair, she had never said a harsh word to Nobuko.

One morning in early spring, while Nobuko was sweeping the garden walks, she heard someone crying softly. She peeked around the corner of the garden wall to find a lovely woman sitting on a stone bench.

Of course, Nobuko recognized the mistress of the house, although she had never met her. The young chore girl meant to quietly retreat, but her feet would not let her. The sounds of the young widow's grief pulled so hard at Nobuko's heart; she could not bring herself to leave. And even though she knew the housekeeper would be angry at her for bothering the young widow, she stepped around the corner and into the garden anyway.

"Pardon me, mistress," Nobuko said from a respectful distance. "Are you well? Is there something I can do to help?"

The young widow turned to look at Nobuko in surprise. Her face was beautiful and perfectly serene, despite the crystal tears sliding down her snow-white cheeks. Suddenly, Nobuko was unsure of her choice to intrude.

"I am sorry, mistress. I did not mean to bother you," she said, lowering her eyes and beginning to back away.

"You have not," the lady assured her. She beckoned Nobuko to come closer. "Who are you child and why are you here?"

"I am the chore girl, mistress. I clean out the ashes and scrub the floors; sweep the walks and beat the rugs; and anything else the head housekeeper asks me to do."

"You are so young though! You must be industrious indeed to be working at such an age." There was a deep sadness in the young widow's gentle voice. "In happier times you would not have had to. You could have explored the little islands and played down by the river's edge as my son liked to do. He would be close to your age, I think. Today is his birthday. He would have been nine years old today."

Nobuko had never seen a boy in the house and her heart ached at the thought of why that might be.

"What is your name, child?" the lady asked her, not unkindly.

"My name is Nobuko, mistress," the young girl answered respectfully.

"You have a caring heart, Nobuko. Here, take these." The beautiful widow handed Nobuko a small paper bag. "They were his favorite. Now go along, I would not wish you to get scolded for falling behind in your work."

Nobuko thanked the lady, gratefully. She slipped the bag into her apron pocket with barely a glance, then taking up her broom, she headed back out into the garden to continue her sweeping.

For the rest of the morning she went about her work, not even taking a moment to peek at the bag, despite her curiosity.

When the sun was high in the sky, Nobuko set aside her broom and bucket and headed home to make lunch for her grandmother, as she did everyday.

When she arrived at their house, she finally took the bag from her apron pocket. It was beautiful! The bright green paper was printed all over with silver waterlilies and swimming in between them were tiny golden fishes. It was by far the finest thing Nobuko had ever owned.

Much to her surprise, when she opened the bag's clever folds, she found five perfect golden cookies!

She left two where they were, deciding to save them for her parents who were out working in the fields. The other three she took out, setting one aside for herself and placing one on the tray next to the small bowl of rice which was her grandmother's lunch. Unsure of what to do with the last one, she put it back into her apron pocket.

A smile lit up her grandmother's weathered face when she ate the cookie. Her cheeks became round and rosy in a way that Nobuko had not seen since she was very little.

"Where did you get such a treat?" her grandmother asked. "I have not tasted these in so long! Golden cookies were always my favorite. You may not remember because you were very young, but every year in the spring, we would have a festival for the River King. The cooks of the great houses on the other side of the river would make bags and bags of these to bring to the festival. Everyone, poor and rich alike, would eat them so that prosperity might be shared by all."

"I have another," Nobuko offered, eager to see her grandmother's face light up again.

"No child, you eat it," she said, smiling fondly. "I have had many in my life-time. But who knows when next you might have the chance!"

"I have one for myself," Nobuko assured her grandmother. "But I put the second one in my pocket to share."

"Keep it there, for later. You might find someone who needs it more," her grandmother said.

Nobuko took a bite of the golden cookie she had set aside for herself. It was delicious! Crispy and crumbly, it melted in her mouth like nothing she had ever eaten before. Now she understood why they had been her grandmother's favorite.

She made sure her grandmother had settled in with her lunch. Then, giving her a kiss on her weathered cheek Nobuko headed back out to finish the afternoon work that waited for her.

The young chore girl made her way back across the wooden walks, watching as the river's sluggish brown water moved slowly just a little way below her feet. She wondered what the river might have looked like, back when they still held festivals for the River King.

In the center of the river was an island, which the wooden walks also crossed over. Nobuko had just reached the other side of it when she saw something flash in the water.

She stopped and peered over the edge of the wooden planks, wondering what it could have been. She looked and looked and for a moment thought she saw the brilliant flash of scales in the murky water below. But with the flick of a tail, it was gone, disappearing down into the lank weeds that covered the river's bottom.

Nobuko waited, hoping to see it again. Its scales had been as bright and shiny as the gold-foil fishes on the clever little bag the young widow had given her. She stayed for longer than she should have. In fact, she waited so long that she had to run as quickly as she could just so that she would not be late back to work.

That afternoon went quickly enough. Nobuko cleaned out the ashes and swept the floors, but all the while her thoughts were of scales the color of new minted coins flashing through the dirty water.

The sun was setting by the time her day's work was done, but she did not hurry home as she usually would. Instead, she walked slowly along the edge of the long wooden bridge, looking down into the water as she went.

Of course, she was hoping to catch another glimpse of the golden fish. When she reached the spot where she had last seen it Nobuko stopped and leaned over the railing as far as she could, watching for flashes of gold in the river weeds. Then suddenly there it was, looking back at her with big gold eyes. With a flick of its tail, the fish swam right up to the surface. And to her amazement, it spoke to her.

"Hello!" it greeted her, its scales gleaming bright in the setting sun. "Are you the same girl I saw earlier today?"

"I am," she admitted because she was a truthful girl.

"What is your name?" asked the fish.

"Nobuko," she answered. "What is yours?"

"Hmm, I don't know that fish usually have names," the fish said.

"Well fish don't usually talk with people either," the young girl pointed out.

"True," the fish agreed. "But when I sleep on the riverbed, I often dream that I am a human. So maybe that's why."

"Maybe," the young girl conceded.

"I'm so glad to have someone to talk to!" the fish said, spinning joyously in the water. "Let's be friends!"

"Okay!" Nobuko agreed, happily. There weren't many children in the village, and besides she had always been so busy working that she had never had the time to make friends. That her first friend was a fish didn't seem odd to her at all. She reached into her apron pocket and took out the golden cookie. She broke off a small piece for herself.

"My grandmother told me they used to make these cookies for the River King's festival. Since we are friends now and you live in the river, it makes sense for us to share it," she said as she tossed the rest of the cookie down to the fish below. The fish caught it and gobbled it up.

"Delicious!" it cried, leaping high out of the water. In fact, it leapt so high out of the water that it landed right on the island's shore.

Horrified, Nobuko rushed back and down the steps that led to the island below, hoping to catch the stranded fish in time to throw it back in the water. Before she could reach it though, there was a shower of glittering scales. Standing there in their midst was a boy, just a little older than her. His skin was golden as were the clothes he wore. Even his dark hair was tipped in gold. He blinked big gold eyes at her once, twice, then with a shout leapt high into the air.

"Haha! Look at me! Look at me! Standing on two legs and all!" he crowed. "Was that a magic cookie you gave me?"

"I don't think so," Nobuko said. "My grandmother and I both ate one and nothing happened to us!"

"Oh well, whatever the reason, at least now we can play together," he said, and grabbed her by the hand. They played until it was nearly too dark for her to see. By then they were back to the place where the pile of scales still sat, gleaming in the deepening twilight.

The boy went to stand in the middle of the shiny mound.

"Will you come to play with me tomorrow?" he asked, and Nobuko agreed that she would.

A glittering whirlwind of scales swirled up around the boy's feet, then with a mighty leap the golden boy was back in the water, a fish once again.

"I'll see you tomorrow!" He said, swimming down into the dark water.

When Nobuko looked down at the place where the boy had stood only a moment before, she found a single golden scale shining on the dark ground. She picked it up and slid it into her pocket where it stayed.

The two children met the next day and every day after that. As soon as Nobuko finished with her work, she would hurry to where he waited at the foot of the bridge. She would share with him one of the rice cakes she had made that morning, saving it from those she had made for her parents to eat while they worked in the fields. They would play until it was almost dark, then afterwards promise to see each other again the next day.

One day, Nobuko finished her work earlier than usual. She met with the golden boy and decided that since they had more time, they should explore the rest of the island. They found many interesting places, but their favorite was a small pool of cold water, clear as crystal. The whole of its sandy bottom glittered in the late afternoon sun. And when they knelt down to see if they could figure out why, they saw that it was covered with thousands and thousands of fish scales.

This went on for some time until the little chore girl and the fish who was sometimes a boy had become fast friends.

One evening just after they had finished playing and after the golden boy had become a fish once again, Nobuko stayed just a little longer talking to him over the edge of the wooden bridge. She had just said goodbye and tossed him the last bit of rice cake from out of her apron pocket when she heard a cold voice say. "What are you doing?"

Nobuko jumped and turned to find the housekeeper standing just behind her. For a moment, the woman's yellow eyes seemed to glow red in the light of the lantern that she was holding. But when Nobuko blinked, the glow disappeared.

Now, Nobuko was a truthful girl, so she admitted to the housekeeper that she had been feeding a fish crumbs that she had saved back from lunch and kept in her pocket. That the fish was also a boy, she kept to herself. Bowing her head she waited for the scolding about wasting food that she was sure to come.

"That is a very kind thing to do," the housekeeper said in the gentlest voice that Nobuko had ever heard her use.

The young chore girl kept her head bowed, at a loss as to what to say.

"I am on my way to see my son," the housekeeper continued." Since it has grown so dark, you are welcome to share my lantern with me."

There was no good reason for Nobuko to refuse such a kind offer. So back along the bridges she walked next to the housekeeper. The tall stern woman, still speaking very kindly to her, expressed her surprise that there were any fish left in the river at all. She asked how it had come about that Nobuko was feeding one.

Again, Nobuko was an honest girl and did not want to lie to the housekeeper. So, she told her about how she had found the young widow, their mistress, in the garden and how she had given Nobuko the bag of golden cookies.

The scolding that Nobuko was convinced would now surely come, did not. Much to her surprise.

"Ah yes, those cookies were her son's favorite," the housekeeper nodded. "Such a tragedy for her to have lost him."

"He died then?" Nobuko asked, the memory of the young widow's sadness tugging at her heart.

"He must have. Though it was before my time as housekeeper, I have been told that he wandered down to the river's edge and has never been seen since."

"That is horrible!" Nobuko exclaimed.

"Yes, horrible," the housekeeper agreed. Her voice was flat, but when Nobuko looked up into her eyes, she saw them shining with tears.

They parted ways at the end of the last bridge, Nobuko turned for home and the housekeeper continued on towards the town gates.

It seemed that luck was with Nobuko because the next day and for the whole week after, she finished her work early. And each time, she rushed off right after to the island to play. The boy who was sometimes a fish would meet her there leaping high up out of the water and transforming in a shower of golden scales. She was so happy to have a friend that she did not worry about much else, but sometimes she would get a little shiver along her spine. And sometimes she thought she saw a pair of pale yellow eyes watching them from just above the river's muddied water. But if she blinked, they would vanish.

One afternoon she went to look for the housekeeper, as she usually did, to tell her that she was finished for the day and to collect her pay. She could not find her anywhere and none of the other servants that she asked had seen her either. She waited for a little longer, her feet itching to be off. Finally, she decided she could not wait any longer, so she left.

She raced along the wooden bridges to the steps that would lead her down to the island. Even before she was at the bottom, she heard a tremendous splash. She ran to the shore just in time to see the golden fish arch high up into the air. Nobuko was horrified to see a monster launch itself out of the water after him. Its hide was the same color as the muddy river. But its pale scaly belly flashed against the dark water as it opened impossibly wide jaws filled with sharp white teeth. The jaws snapped closed, but they missed the golden fish who had slipped back into the water and hid down in the river weeds. The creature launched itself out of the water again and again as the golden fish darted in and out of hiding.

Nobuko did not think, she picked up stones from at her feet and began to throw them as hard as she could at the creature, aiming for its bulging eyes.

Now Nobuko might have been a young girl, but she was strong from all the hard work she had done, and the stones were sharp. The creature stopped its thrashing and slowly sank below the water, its sickly yellow eyes watching Nobuko the whole time. On her part, Nobuko did not stop throwing stones until the telltale ripples had moved far, far away.

Not knowing what to do but sure that the golden fish who was sometimes a boy would not make an appearance at the shore she was on, Nobuko headed to their secret spring. The last of the afternoon light sparkled on the cold water as she washed the dirt from her hands and the tears that she had not even known she had shed from her face. She was surprised to hear a familiar joyful voice behind her.

"What was that!" the golden boy exclaimed.

She was so happy to see him safe, she hugged him. "I don't know! But I feel like maybe it has been watching us and that was a trap you just swam into. Maybe, maybe... we shouldn't meet anymore." Nobuko had a hard time getting the words out. She did not want to lose her only friend.

"No!" the boy stamped his foot. "I don't want to," he added in a sad, quiet voice.

"I don't want to either," admitted Nobuko. "I know! We could meet earlier, after I make my grandmother's lunch. And we can meet here instead of our usual spot. Maybe then, the monster won't see you."

"Then that is what we will do!" the golden boy whooped exuberantly, leaping high into the air.

They said goodbye and the boy promised to be careful.

All through the night Nobuko worried about the fish who was sometimes a boy. She fell asleep with the golden fish scale that she had found at their first meeting clutched tightly in her hand.

The next morning, it was the cook who gave her her tasks for the day, but Nobuko was so preoccupied she did not think much of it. She finished the them as quickly as she could and rushed back to make her grandmother lunch.

While they were eating, she asked her grandmother, "Grandmother, have you ever heard of a monster living in the river?"

"You have not heard the story?" her grandmother asked in turn. Nobuko shook her head.

"Long ago, when my mother was a young girl and our town was still beautiful and prosperous, a demon came up from a delta far to the south.

"They say the demon was the son of a powerful sorceress. It had long jaws, filled with pointed teeth, which opened so wide they could snap up a whole bull calf, which it did more than once. And its scaly hide was so tough, no arrows could pierce it. But most terrifying was that it could move beneath the water so silently a person would never even know that it was there. Only occasionally would one see its yellow eyes above the water and in lantern light they were said to glow red." Nobuko continued to listen with a quailing heart as her grandmother told the story. "It took to stealing beautiful young women away from the town as well as from the families across the river. Finally, the elders of the village made the long trek to the head of the river. There they made an offering to the River King in the hopes that he could help.

"On the very next day, there was a great storm and when it had ended the monster was dead. Many of the villagers insisted that they had seen the River King himself, dressed all in his golden armor, kill the demon and toss his body up on the shore."

"But grandmother, is this a true story or just a children's tale?" She asked, heart trembling.

"Oh, it is true! The demon's hide still hangs on the town gates to this day."

Nobuko knew that she had to tell this story to the boy. "I am sorry grandmother, I must go!" she exclaimed as she jumped up and ran out the door.

Her feet pounded on the wooden bridges as she ran all the way to the island and flew down the steps. But despite her fears, all seemed quiet. No sinister shadows darkened the sluggish river; no nacred yellow eyes peered up from the muddy water. Nobuko's heart began to slow.

She headed towards the spring where she had promised to meet the fish who was sometimes a boy. Someone was already there when she arrived, but it was not the someone she had expected.

Sitting on a large stone at the edge of the spring was Nobuko's mistress, the young widow. She was looking into the spring with a wistful expression and a sad smile on her lips.

Nobuko did not know what to do! She did not want to intrude on her mistress, but she was supposed to meet the boy here.

As she stood there unsure whether she should stay or go, the young widow glanced up right at her. She smiled.

"Hello again!" Her voice was just as kind as Nobuko remembered, though perhaps a little less sad than it had been last time. Nobuko bowed and dropped her eyes respectfully.

"Now, now," the young widow said, "There is no need to be so formal here. This is a special place, my wishing place, where a person can be whoever they want to be. At least, that is what he used to tell me." She patted a stone next to the one where she sat. "Come sit with me."

Nobuko did as the young widow asked. She looked up at the lady's beautiful face which was turned towards the spring with its glittering bottom covered in fish scales clear to see beneath the crystal water.

"When I was young, I would come here to escape from my teachers. I met a boy here, a beautiful boy with eyes the color of fine tea and hair as black as the night sky. He did not live in the town, but further upriver. We always met here around the time of the River King's Festival. He would tell me stories of the river and we would laugh and make wishes while we threw the fish scales that he had brought with him into the spring.

"But I was the daughter of a rich family, and he just a common fish peddler. One year after he had left, I was married to the son of another influential family. That next year I was with child. Even so, I came to the spot where we had met so often, to tell him the news. My heart felt as though it would break, for you see, I had secretly been in love with him. But he did not come. Not that year, nor any other year since.

"I lost my husband only a year after our son was born and soon after my son disappeared as well. Still, I come here every year at this time to dream of once was and make wishes."

Nobuko watched the silent tears flow freely down the young widow's silken cheeks. She was a compassionate girl and her heart broke at the sight. Without thinking, she took the young widow's hand in hers.

The young widow turned to Nobuko. "I would make a wish for you sweet child if I could, but I have no fish scale to make a wish with," she lamented.

Nobuko pulled the golden fish scale out from the apron pocket where she always kept it. She offered it to the young widow beside her, but the kind woman shook her head and would not take it.

"No, you should make a wish," the young widow insisted, so Nobuko threw the golden scale into the clear water. It glittered as it slowly sank to join all the other wishes on the bottom.

But Nobuko, being the tenderhearted girl that she was, had not made one small wish for herself but rather she had made one big wish.

When the scale came to rest at the bottom of the spring the whole island shook as though a giant had stamped his foot. The water sprayed up in a cascade of diamonds and in its midst stood a beautiful man dressed in robes of mercurial blue with hair as black as the night sky and fine tea-colored eyes.

At that same moment, there was a tremendous splash and from the other side of the island raced the boy who was sometimes a fish running full tilt in a swirl of golden scales. And after him came the same terrifying creature she had seen the day before. Its short legs propelled it at an amazing speed as it thrashed through the trees, its thick tail felling them in its wake. Its monstrous body shifted as it chased him, changing into the tall angular form of the housekeeper.

"You shall not escape me again!" she roared.

The boy leapt high into the air landing in the spring just as the man was stepping out of it. The golden scales flew around the tall figure settling on his blue robes until he was clothed in shining armor.

"I thought you had gone for good, River King," the sorceress (for that was who she was) said in a guttural hiss. "You killed my son, so I came for the son of your heart's love. But why should I settle for a little fish when the king of them all stands before me."

"All that stands before you sorceress is your death!" the River King boomed.

A great storm howled down from the sky. Lightning flashed across the clouds, the wind screamed, and the storm raged. Trees crashed and splintered around them while Nobuko, the young widow, and the boy who was sometimes a fish cowered in terror. A horrendous battle ensued as the River King, resplendent in his armor, fought the sorceress who had once again become a monstrous demon. The three of them held tight to each other and the stone next to which they huddled as a wall of water rushed over the island.

When at last the storm quieted, they opened their eyes to find the River King still standing. At his feet, the sorceress lay dead pierced through by a thousand fish scales.

The young widow stood up, her eyes wide with joy and surprise. She looked down at the boy, who was still a boy, then up at the River King. "You have returned."

The River King came over and took up her hands in his. "We have."

And so, Nobuko's wish had come true. The river had been washed clean again. The young widow's love had returned to her, though it turned out that he was anything but a common fisherboy. And the boy who had sometimes been a fish, but it turned out had always been a boy in truth, was safe.

The River King had never stopped coming to the island, as the young widow had thought. But seeing her happy and with a beautiful son had chosen to watch from afar. That was, until the sorceress thought cursing the son of the woman he loved would be a fitting revenge for the death of her own son.

To save him, the River King had transformed the boy into a fish and himself in the golden scales that protected him. Which was how the sorceress was able to take power from the river and keep the River King weak. Soon both the River King and the boy had forgotten who they had been. That was until the boy ate the cookie Nobuko had given him and began to remember what it was to be human.

From that day on, the town grew prosperous again. Nobuko and the boy who was no longer a fish stayed friends. Nobuko's family became caretakers of the young widow's estate.

As for the young widow, she married the River King who came to visit whenever the moon shone on the water. And when her son, now a grown man, came of age, she and the River King went off in a boat made of mist to live in the River King's home. But every year they returned for the River Festival bringing with them loads of golden cookies.

"Helping someone remember who they truly are is admirable indeed," said the Green sister as she too added her thread to the weaving. "And certainly, there is nothing more precious than a loyal friend.

"I have heard a tale that tells of this very thing. It is about a young girl, and it all starts one Christmas morning..."

The Green Sister's Tale

The Rocking Horse

When the children woke on Christmas morning, they found piles of presents under the tree. There was something for everyone: George had his clockwork mice and Teddy his paint set. There was a working train, complete with bright red caboose, for William, and a silver comb and mirror for Sarah. And for Nell a tea set of her very own, packed neatly in a picnic basket for her to take out on her adventures. However, everyone agreed that the grandest gift of all was the great black rocking horse that stood at the far end of the nursery.

What a fine, proud head he had! And the rippling mane that fell from his high-crested neck was so long and full, it nearly touched the ground. The tiny golden bells which hung from his saddle and reins chimed merrily with each graceful sway of the rocking horse's head. A small brass plate affixed to his bridle proclaimed his name to be Roland.

The children, one and all, hugged the creature's beautiful neck and stroked its soft nostrils. They, each one, kissed the broad forehead between its eyes. And what eyes those were! Great eyes, the color of fire which shone so wonderfully bright, they seemed as though they were truly alive. As if, at any moment, they would blink and look around. They did not of course, they only continued to stare fixedly ahead.

Each child took turns riding on the great creature's back; its swaying gate carrying them off bravely into battle, or into the wild unknown of frontiers as yet unexplored and landscapes unseen. He was their gallant charger, elegant palfrey, or loyal pack horse.

But eventually the children's interest waned. George returned to his clockwork mice and Teddy to his paint set. William gathered up his train and set off in search of places to set its tracks and Sarah used her silver comb to brush her doll's hair. One by one they all drifted away, all except Nell.

She loved Roland dearly. All day long she sat upon his back, rocking furiously as she imagined them riding through wildflower meadows and along rainbow streams flowing beneath sherbet-colored skies.

In fact, Nell was having so much fun with Roland that she forgot about dinner entirely. And when bedtime came, she had to be lifted from the saddle, having fallen asleep with her arms wrapped tightly around the rocking horse's neck.

So, it should come as no surprise that after having missed dinner she was quite hungry when she woke later that night. She slipped from her warm bed and padded down the hall towards the stairs that led to the kitchen.

As she passed the nursery door she paused, having a great desire to check on Roland. She longed to see the grand creature with his splendid, rippling tail and great fiery eyes, just for a moment.

When she opened the door, she was surprised to find the corner where he had been empty. The soft chiming of bells drew her eyes to the other side of the nursery. There Roland stood in front of the large windows, as though he watched the stars in the sky high above. Nell wondered how he had gotten there and went over to see, resting her hand on the soft black nose. When she looked up into the rocking horse's eyes, she found them full of tears. One fell, silvery bright onto her hand, where it lay warm and real.

"Oh, my poor Roland, why are you crying?" she asked.

"Because I miss my home, sweet Nell," Roland answered. "I can hear my mares and foals whinnying to me as they race over the hills."

"Why don't you go to them?" the girl asked.

"Because I am bound here, and so cannot leave," the rocking horse replied.

"You are a prisoner?" Nell said. It broke her heart to see her gentle, patient Roland sad. So even though she would miss him terribly, she opened the window so that he might go back to the home he so clearly loved.

"Ah, Nell you are so kind. Thank you," he said. "But I do not wish to leave you either, for we have had such a wonderful time together. Search through my mane until you find a silver hair. There will be only one. Pluck it and wear it round your finger. When the dawn comes, open the window and call my name and I will return to you happily."

She searched through his mane, and found a single silver hair, just as Roland had said. She plucked it and braided it to make a ring for her finger. The rocking horse nodded his head once, then with a joyous ringing of bells, he lifted up into the air. Through the nursery window he flew, racing out across the starry night sky, high up over the moon-silvered clouds, heading towards his home in Rocking Horse Land.

Nell went back to bed, her rumbling tummy forgotten. She ran her finger over the silver ring of Roland's hair until she fell asleep and began to dream of Rocking Horse Land. She could see them all racing over emerald hills as smooth as glass. Their proud heads nodding, up and down, up and down, in that particular way that rocking horses do, as they strove to go faster, shining manes streaming out behind them with their speed. Their coats flashed as one by one they raced by: silvery dapples, coppery chestnuts and golden cremellos. And in front of them all, was the ebony figure of her beloved Roland.

Nell was up before dawn to make sure the nursery window was open. She called Roland's name out into the pale morning light. And there he was, dipping and dancing through the fading shadows. He floated through the open window and landed at her feet.

"Did you have fun, my dearest Roland?" she asked.

"Yes, my sweet Nell, it was wonderful! Oh, thank you, thank you, thank you!" and with that, he was still. His limbs rigid once more as his eyes stared fixedly ahead, just as one would expect a rocking horse to be.

Nell returned to the nursery again that night and every night after, to open the window for Roland. Every morning he returned as promised, so that he might carry Nell off on her adventures the whole day long.

Another Christmas morning came around, and again the children were greeted with brightly wrapped presents waiting for them under the tree.

George got a clockwork cat to chase his clockwork mice, and Teddy finally had an easel to hold up his canvases. William got little houses and stores with people to set up alongside his train's tracks, and Sarah finally got the pair of long gloves she had wished for all year long, the ones with tiny pearl buttons. But it was Nell's gift which was the most unexpected.

It came in the form of a lovely white pony and from that day on they went everywhere together.

Still, every night Nell would remember to open the window for Roland. And sometimes if the weather was foul or if she just had a mind to, she would go to the nursery to sit on his back, rocking to and fro as she told him of her latest adventures.

Eventually there were other children; younger brothers and sisters who hugged Roland's beautiful neck and kissed him between his great fiery eyes. They would ride on his strong back and make up adventures of their own. And they began to leave the window open for Roland at night.

There came a time when Nell realized it had been some while since she had last visited the nursery. So that evening, she quietly padded down the hall and peaked in the door. She found Roland standing at the window staring forlornly out at the trees swaying in the night wind. His bridle was missing a bell or three and his mane and tail were perhaps not as full as they had once been. Yet he was still beautiful, and his great eyes still shone brightly.

"Ah, sweet Nell, have you finally remembered me?" he asked, and though his voice was sad, it held no blame in it.

"My wonderful, patient Roland, I am so sorry!" she exclaimed as she hugged his neck and stroked his long soft muzzle. "You gave me so many happy memories, shared so many of my dreams and kept all my confidences. I love you so, but I see now that it is past time I set you free. Be well my dear Roland." With that she opened the window.

The great rocking horse swayed, dipping his head so deeply that it nearly touched the floor, and then with a jubilant ringing of bells, he sprang out into the night sky.

Nell unwound the band of silver that circled her finger and let the evening breeze carry it away to follow behind the one who had gifted it to her. She thought that she could hear the sound of joyous whinnying; a welcoming home to one long lost. Smiling, she quietly closed the window and locked it.

The Blue sister wiped a tear from her eye at the end of the Green sister's story. "Ah, sweet Roland to have waited so patiently even though he longed for home! I too have a story of love, and a longing so deep it could fill the sea." She drew a strand of sapphire thread through her fingers and added it to the weave as she began her tale.

The Blue Sister's Tale

Daughter of the Sea

There was once a young fisherman and his wife who lived in a cottage at the edge of the sea. The life they had chosen was not easy, but they were happy in each other's company and content in all things save one, they did not have a child.

This thought was ever on the young fishwife's mind. It made it so that she rarely slept and could most often be found walking along the shore, with only the light of the moon and stars above her. With each passing day her heart grew heavier, until one fateful night, it seemed too much for her to bear. She began to walk out into the sea, resolved to let the waves drag her down into that forever sleep. But just as her foot touched the water, she heard a soft cry.

The sound caught her ear, and she turned away from the ocean, walking along its edge instead until she came to a tidal pool. There, swaddled in seaweed, she found a tiny baby girl. A necklace hung around her neck and on it was a shimmering scale.

The young wife brushed the baby's soft cheek. The baby cooed happily at her and she knew right then that she could not leave the babe there all alone. So she took the child, although she was not sure whether it was the right thing to do. She cuddled it close as she carried it away from the sea, back towards the little cottage she shared with her husband.

Time passed. And as will often happen, the young fisherman and his wife grew to be an old fisherman and wife. And their daughter, for that is what they told people, grew as well.

The couple had been gifted with three fine sons over the years, all of which they were very proud of. Still, the child the sea had given them was their only daughter and the fisherman's wife loved her dearly.

The girl had grown to be a lovely young maid, with wild dark hair and eyes as gray as storm-tossed waves. Her mouth was generous, and she often smiled. But of all those things, it was her voice for which she was best known. For no one who had ever heard her sing could forget it. And she often sang while she walked along the shore, gathering seaweed for her mother's soup and searching for treasures in the sand.

That was exactly what she was doing one day while a storm brewed overhead, its dark roiling clouds turning everything to the color of slate. The waves bucked wildly along the sand, cresting high above the sea, before crashing down into mountains of foam. The wind was blowing full in her face, stinging with salt and sand.

This bothered the fisherman's daughter not at all. She laughed at the wild ocean and sang with the frigid wind as it stroked her cheek and tangled her hair. She continued on her way happily down the strand.

She thought herself alone until, to her surprise, she saw a milk white horse some little ways ahead, standing in the waves and sea spray. It was long and lean. And its mane and tail hung lank and dripping with sea water.

Although she was curious, she did not think too much of it. After all, it was not uncommon for a horse to wander along the shore.

But this horse did not wander, instead its head was turned towards her, as if waiting. And when she walked past him, he turned to follow at her side. When she reached out towards him, he did not shy away, just continued walking beside her. He had such a gentlemanly manner that she felt it safe to rest her hand on his shoulder; the coat beneath her fingers was short, and as soft as seal fur

They walked companionably down the beach until they reached the sea cliffs that pointed like a giant's finger out into the storm tossed water.

There the horse stopped and turned to look at her. His eyes, green as beryls, regarded her for a moment before bowing his head to her. Then he turned and with a flick of his tail, trotted out into the iron gray sea. She watched in amazement as he was swallowed up by the waves.

She was still standing there when the next wave washed up, leaving behind a large fish on the sand at her feet.

She carried the fish home to her family, who marveled at it and asked how she had come across it. She told them, for they were not generally a family to keep secrets, save one. That one secret, the wife kept close to her heart, along with the scale necklace, listening as her daughter told her tale but saying nothing in return.

The next day the fisherman's wife gave her daughter a long list of chores, in the hopes of keeping her home. But before midday the girl was back down at the water's edge, walking amongst the foam and singing sweetly to the sea.

The white horse met her again on the shore. He walked along beside her as she rested her hand on his shoulder and left her when they reached the sea cliffs as he had before. The wave that followed after his leaving carried with it a fish even bigger than the last. The young woman brought it home with her.

It was the most wonderful fish, with tender white flesh. But as they sat down to eat it for their dinner that night, the fisherman's wife could not keep the worry from her face.

"You say this white horse is always a gentleman and asks nothing in return for the fine fish he gives us. But that doesn't mean that it will always be so," she warned her daughter. "What he may ask, I cannot say. But promise me that you will never mount upon his back, no matter how tempting it may be. If you do, he will surely carry you down below the waves, and I fear your feet will never again touch the land."

The girl promised her mother that she would be careful and not give in to such a temptation.

Yet, despite her mother's warning, she was down at the sea shore the next day, her basket full of seaweed. Again, the milk white horse was waiting for her on the sand. They walked amiably together as they had the day before, save this time she did not sing.

When they reached the spot where they would usually part ways, the great white horse stepped out in front, turning his warm side towards her. He nickered and pushed at her hip, urging her to mount on his back. Laughing, she spun away from the circle of his neck.

"Oh no, my handsome one," she admonished, shaking her finger at him. "I will not ride on your back, for I know where that will take me!"

The horse nickered and shook his mane at her, before turning and walking out into the crashing waves.

This time, the fish that washed up on the next wave was so big, she had to run and get her father and brothers to carry it home.

As they ate that evening the fisherman's wife asked her daughter if the sea horse had indeed offered her a ride.

"He did, but have no fear," she reassured her mother. "I kept my promise and did not mount on his back when he asked me. Which I am sure you have guessed, for here I sit, and I doubt I shall see him again."

But the fisherman's wife was not so sure, and feared she may yet lose her daughter.

The next day, the young woman went with her basket down to the sea, as she always did. And despite what she had said to her mother, she kept watch for the milk white horse. She did not find him, but that wasn't to say the beach was empty. Standing in the very place where the milk-white horse would usually be, was a man.

He was tall and lean, with skin as white as alabaster and hair like a night-dark sea. As she drew closer, he bowed most politely, and the eyes that met hers as he rose were also as green as beryls.

He introduced himself as the Sea King's son, his seventh son to be precise. And though it sounded fantastical, she found she did not doubt him. He asked if he could walk with her, and she agreed.

As they walked, he told her about his home beneath the waves. Of his father's castle with its towers of pearl and its gardens filled with coral trees and anemones, over which jellyfish hung like lanterns. He talked of nights filled with whale song, and days spent along the ocean's sandy floor, playing hide and seek with seals through giant kelp forests.

She found her feet moving slower, reluctant for the walk to end, but end it did. They parted ways when they reached the sea cliffs, but not before he had gotten her promise to meet again the next day.

He left her with a bow, and turning, he walked away, out into the rolling waves. The sea swallowed him up, just as it had the white horse. Again, a giant wave washed up on the shore, leaving a present at her feet. Except this time it was no fish that she found on the sand. In its stead, were twelve perfect oysters. She gathered them up in her basket and carried them home. When they were opened up that night for dinner they found, much to their surprise, that each one held a silvery white pearl.

The fisherman's wife watched her daughter with worried eyes as they all sat down to eat. Her daughter had not said from where the oysters had come, and the wife did not ask; afraid she in turn would have to tell her own secret.

The next day, the young woman kept her promise to meet the Sea King's son. And when she came home that night, she had twelve more oysters, all with pearls even bigger than the ones before. And the fishwife's heart grew ever more uneasy.

When next the fisherman's daughter and the Sea King's son met, the sun shone brightly down on them. Its warm light tipped every wave in diamonds as they walked hand in hand along the sparkling shore. When they reached the sea cliffs, the Sea King's son stopped and taking both her hands in his laughingly stole a kiss. "Come with me," he said in a voice filled with delight. "Be my wife. I want to show you all that I have spoken of, and more."

"Come with you? How can I?" she said. "I would die if I followed you beneath the waves!"

"Die? I dare say you would not! You are a daughter of the sea. I knew it when first I heard you sing," he insisted earnestly. "Though for the life of me, I can't say where you have hidden your tail."

His words made no sense, though she wished with all her heart that they were true. She shook her head no, and sadness filled his beautiful green eyes.

"It was your song that called me out of the sea," he confessed. "I came only with the hope that you would be my bride. But my time here is not without end; I must leave on the spring tide to return to my father's kingdom beneath the waves. I do not know when or if I can return."

"The spring tide!" she said, and her heart felt as heavy as lead. "But that is tomorrow."

"Just so, my siren," he said sadly. "Meet me here if you can, before I leave."

He did not wait for her answer but turned and left. As she watched him disappear into the ocean's embrace, she knew her cheeks were wet with more than sea spray.

When her daughter did not return for supper, the fisherman's wife feared the worst. She went down to the shore to search for her and found her there in the shadow of the sea cliffs, her face wet with tears.

"Oh, child what is wrong!" she asked, although in her heart she already knew.

Her daughter did not answer, so the fisherman's wife threw her shawl about the weeping girl's shoulders and led her home.

All through dinner, her daughter said not a word, and everyone watched her with worried eyes.

That night while on her way to her own bed, the fisherman's wife checked the house as she usually did only to find that her daughter's bed was empty.

She found the girl on the front stoop sitting in the full moon's light, listening to the waves crash on the not so distant shore. She was crying softly to herself.

The fisherman's wife sat down on the stoop next to her daughter. Putting her arms around the girl, she asked what it was that made her cry so. Her daughter told her all about the Sea King's son and all that he had said besides. Hugging her mother tight as she admitted how much she wanted to be his bride, even if it meant that it would be her death to which she went.

The wife's heart broke and she knew she could keep her secret no longer. She drew the necklace out from where she kept it hid. Setting the shimmering scale in her daughter's hand, she told her of how she had found her swaddled in seaweed out on the strand. When she had finished the telling, she kissed the girl on her forehead then went to her own bed, knowing that her daughter would be gone with the next tide.

The morning dawned bright and clear. Never had the fisherman's wife seen such a gloriously blue sky. Still her heart was heavy as she began her day.

A little later, the men of the house came back from their run, their boat so full of fish it could hardly float. The whole village turned out to help them with their haul, and there was more than enough for everyone. But the fisherman's wife was not there.

When the evening came and the fisherman went to look for his wife, he did not find her at home. Instead, he found her standing at the edge of the lapping waves, her shawl drawn tight around her as she stared out across the water. Tears were flowing freely down her cheeks, and at her feet sat a small chest filled to overflowing with jewels and gold coins.

He held his wife and stroked her hair, his cheeks as wet as hers. They both had known that the day might come when their daughter would have to return to the sea. Still their hearts were heavy.

From then on, the village prospered. Never again having to worry about missing boats or empty nets. The jewels and gold went to setting the fisherman and his wife up in comfort, and to making sure their sons each had a boat of their own.

A few years passed, and although the wife loved her husband and sons dearly, she greatly missed her daughter. She took to walking along the strand as she had done before, and sometimes her husband would join her.

On one such night, when the moon was at her fullest, they heard someone softly singing. They followed the song, and there, at the foot of the sea cliffs, they found a small girl child waiting. She was wrapped in a seaweed blanket, and about her neck hung a necklace, just the same as her mother had worn. The scale it held shimmered in the moon's bright light.

Happily, they scooped the girl up and headed home, their hearts full once again.

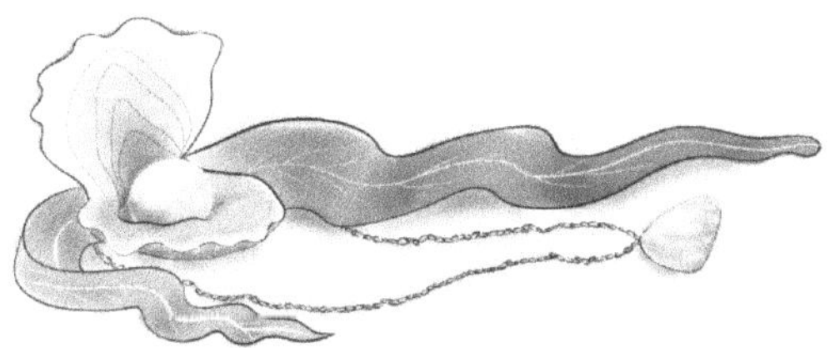

"To let someone go for love, is truly love indeed," said the Indigo sister as she wove her thread deftly into the weave. "But sometimes love needs to be followed and that takes heart and determination. I have heard of such a tale, and it all started when a king lost his way..."

The Indigo Sister's Tale

The Raven's Bride

It happened one day that the king was out hunting in a great wood when, through no fault of his own, he was separated from his huntsmen. On and on he rode, becoming less sure of his way as the trees crowded closer and closer together. Soon the branches above him were thick enough to block out the sky and the wood became as dark as night.

As he came around a bend, he found a great dark raven on the path before him. It stood nearly as tall as the king's horse, and its feathers were as black as soot. The eyes that regarded the king glowed like burning coals.

"Where are you headed, your majesty?" asked the Raven.

"I can not say," the king replied, "for I am not sure where I am. In fact, I am quite lost."

"Ah, I can help you," the Raven assured him. "I will lead you out of this wood, if you will consent to give your golden-haired daughter to me as my bride."

Now the king had three daughters, all of which were beautiful. But it was his second daughter, Aurelina, of whom the raven spoke for she was often called Princess Golden-hair. And truly, her hair was as bright as spun gold.

Of course, the king refused.

"As you will," said the Raven. "But I promise, you will not find your way from this wood without me."

Again, the king refused.

The Raven nodded. "Well good luck to you then, and if you change your mind you have only to call out to me and I will be there. But do not take too long or there will nothing left of you for me to lead out." And with that, the Raven flew off.

The king wandered for three days, and the truth of the Raven's words bore out, for no matter how far he went he could not find his way out of the dark wood. Hungry, thirsty, and fearing for his kingdom, the king relented, calling out to the Raven.

As promised, the Raven appeared.

"If my daughter were to become your bride, do you promise no harm will come to her? And that you will take care of her and treat her well?" the king asked. When the Raven assured him that it would be so, the king agreed to give the Raven his daughter as a bride. With that the Raven spread his great wings and bade the king follow as he took to the sky. The king did so and true to his word, the Raven lead him safely out of the forest.

"I will come for my bride tomorrow," the Raven said before flying back toward the wood.

The morning found the Raven waiting outside the castle gates. But when the time came, the king could not bring himself to give up his daughter. So, he had the swineherd's daughter dressed in one of the princess's dresses and sent her out in her stead. After all, the king reasoned with himself, a raven would not be able to tell the difference between a swineherd's daughter and a princess.

The Raven flew away with the swineherd's daughter on his back. On and on he flew, over flowering meadows and rolling hills and great wide rivers, until he finally brought her to a rude hut perched atop a bleak cliff. There was not a soul to be seen for miles, only a great flock of birds of all different kinds wheeling above the hut's meager roof.

There the Raven landed. "Here is our home," he said and bade the girl go in and refresh herself.

When she went inside, she found a wooden table. On it was a golden goblet of good red wine, a silver cup of cider and a earthenware jug full of bitter beer. Tired and concerned for her future, the swineherd's daughter went straight for what she knew. Picking up the earthenware jug of bitter beer, she took a long drink. It was then that the Raven knew it wasn't the princess who stood before him, for what princess would be content with a jug of bitter beer when a golden goblet of good red wine was at hand?

"Come, I will return you to your home for you are not the bride I seek," said the Raven and bade her climb on his back. Away he flew, back over the flowering meadows and rolling hills and great wide rivers until he was once again at the castle gates.

"King!" the Raven boomed in a great voice. "This is not the bride I seek, send out my true bride as we agreed or you and your people will suffer for it!"

The king felt a shiver of fear run down his back for he did not doubt what the Raven said. "Come tomorrow and you will have your true bride," promised the king.

When the morning came, the Raven was once again waiting outside the castle gates. Still, the king found that he could not bring himself to give up his daughter. Instead, he had the steward's daughter dress in one of the princess's dresses and sent her out to meet the Raven. After all, the king reasoned with himself, a steward's daughter is fine enough for a raven.

So, the Raven took the steward's daughter on his back, and away they flew, back to the isolated little hut on the bleak clifftop. Into the hut went the steward's daughter, where she found the wooden table with its golden goblet of red wine, silver cup of cider and earthenware jug of bitter beer. Tired and concerned for her future, the steward's daughter went straight for what she knew. Picking up the silver cup of cider, she took a long drink. It was then that the Raven knew it wasn't the princess who stood before him. For what princess would be content with cider when good red wine was at hand?

"Come," said the Raven, "back we go again, for you are not the bride I seek."

So, the Raven flew back to the castle carrying the steward's daughter with him. When he landed, he called out in a great and terrible voice. All who heard it shivered with unreasoning fear, gooseflesh rising up along their skin as if someone had just walked over their grave.

"So king, this is how you would treat with me! You promise me one bride and send out another. Tomorrow I will come for my true bride and if you do not send her out I will bring the castle down around your head and pick the eyes from your skull!" With that dire warning still ringing through the air, the Raven flew away. But all who had heard him knew he would be back the next morning.

The king realized there was no way around his promise. When he went to his daughter, Aurelina, and told her of the bargain she was quite understandably upset. The rest of the day and night she sat weeping in her chambers. Her sisters' sat with her, comforting her as best they could. But truth be told, deep in their heart of hearts each of them was relived that it was not herself who was to be the Raven's bride.

The day dawned clear and bright. Princess Aurelina's hair was a rippling sheet of gold in the morning sun as she climbed onto the Raven's back, her eyes still red rimmed from weeping the day before. The great Raven spread his wings and carried her up into the sky. Aurelina did not see all the land that they passed over, her eyes still filled with tears. When they reached the rude little hut with its flock of birds wheeling overhead, she was so tired from weeping that she did not wait but slid down from the Raven's back straight away and went into the tiny hut. Seeing the golden goblet of good red wine on the table, she went to it and drank, without even a second thought as to how such a thing would come be in a crude little hut in the first place.

Wonder of wonders, as soon as she drank from the golden goblet the little hut began to grow and change, transforming into a great castle. Its walls were made of alabaster and its rooftops were of silver. The flock of birds that had been circling in the air above changed as well, becoming courtiers and servants and men-at-arms. They all cheered as they gathered around the princess and the Raven. But the Raven was no longer there. In its stead stood a man, tall and fine, wearing an elegant coat. His hair was as black as the raven's feathers. However unlike the raven, his eyes did not glow like burning coals, but instead were a warm, lovely hazel.

"You were the bride I sought," he said taking her hands in his. "It was only when you drank from the golden goblet that my people and I were released from the evil spell placed on us by my stepmother. And now I can ask you properly, will you marry me?"

The princess agreed and so their courtship began. Aurelina could not have wished for more, for the Raven King was very thoughtful and kind to his bride-to-be. They spent many a happy day in each other's company. But as the time for their wedding drew closer, Aurelina found that she missed her father and sisters, and she said as much to the Raven King, sharing with him her desire to visit them.

"Only misfortune will come from such a visit," he warned, clearly troubled. "But I would see you happy, so if you are set on this course, I can not deny you.

So the princess made ready for her trip. Before she left, her husband-to-be gifted her with a napkin made of the finest linen.

"If there is anything you want, anything at all, spread this napkin out on the ground and wish for it and straight away it shall appear. There is only one thing you must never wish for," he cautioned. "You must never wish for me to appear. If you do, misfortune will come of it and there will be a price to pay."

So Aurelina set off to her father's house in a lovely ebony coach pulled by four silver-gray horses. She was accompanied by a full retinue of courtiers and servants, all dressed in the livery of the Raven King's house. They made a splendid sight, and it was not long before her father and sisters heard about the grand lady that traveled through their land. Weren't they surprised when it turned out to be the very same princess they had thought lost to them.

Her father, the king, was so happy to see her! And to hear about the fine husband she was to have and the grand home they lived in. It gladdened his heart to know that his daughter had come out the better for the bad deal that he had been forced to make. Her sisters, however, soon tired of hearing about how wonderfully kind, thoughtful, and handsome their sister's husband-to-be was. (And to be honest, Aurelina did go on a bit more than was polite, finding that she missed her betrothed terribly.) But it was not truly her chatter that turned her sisters' hearts against her. Rather it was that they were secretly envious of her happiness. Each feeling that she might have had this for herself if only the Raven King had asked for her instead of their sister.

"Yes, yes, such a wonderful husband you'll have," said her elder sister. "Almost too good to be believed."

"True!" her younger sister agreed. "Why is he not here with you then, dear sister? It makes one wonder."

And so they went on, their words subtle and spiteful. After several days of this, it became too much for Aurelina to bear. So, even though he had warned her against it, she laid the napkin on the ground and wished for the Raven King to appear.

No sooner had she wished it, but there he stood. And her sisters had nothing to say then, because he was all that they had been told and more. But he did not look at anyone else, only Aurelina and his face was both angry and sad.

"I told you there would be a price to pay if you called me to you and now we will both pay it. A *geas* is on me and I have no choice but to go and I cannot bring you with me, though my heart might break from it. I doubt you will see me again," that said he stooped to pick up the napkin on which he stood and was a raven once more. Spreading his great wings, he flew off.

At the same time, Aurelina's fine ebony coach vanished, and all of her retinue changed into birds once more. They flew off as well, following their master. But, Aurelina paid no attention to that save to note what direction they flew off in. Without a word to her sisters, she tucked up her skirts and headed off the way she had seen her beloved go, determined to find him despite his dire prediction.

She walked and walked the whole day through until she could walk no more, then she laid herself down to rest. She woke the next morning and set out again. Every day she searched, asking all she met if they had seen a great black raven flying overhead and if they had, what direction he might have gone in. But no one could tell her a thing. This went on for quite some time till it seemed to Aurelina that she had walked the whole world round. Then one day, just as night was falling, she came to a hut at the edge of a wood. Unable to put one foot in front of the other, she knocked on the door not caring who it was that might answer.

The door opened and there stood an old woman with cloud-white hair and a kindly face.

"Child, you should not be here," said the old woman. "This is Death's house, and it would do you no good if he were to find you here. He spares none, young or old, fair or foul. I should know, I am his grandmother."

But Aurelina, beyond caring, found that she could not walk another step. Death's grandmother, seeing how tired she was, took pity on the princess. She offered her food and drink, and while they ate, Aurelina told the old woman everything that had happened. The old woman admired her determination to find the sweetheart she had lost.

"There may be somewhat that I can do to help you," she said. "Do you see the clock in the corner there? When you have done eating, climb into it and be very quiet. When my grandson returns home, we will see if he knows something which might help you in your quest."

Aurelina did as the old woman suggested. It was

no trouble for her to hide in the clock, for it was a huge old thing that filled the corner of the room and could have fit three of her inside with room to spare.

It was not long before she heard the door open and close. The air around her became frigid and it took all that she had to keep her teeth from chattering.

"Hello Grandmother!" Death said and she shivered to hear his voice. "Phew... I smell mortal blood in this house for sure!"

"Nonsense!" exclaimed his grandmother. "Mortal blood indeed! As if a mortal would come to this house if they had anywhere else to go! Though I did have quite the dream today. Sit down and eat, and I will tell you all about it."

The princess could hear the scrape of the chair as Death sat down to dinner and the clank of silverware as he ate. As for herself, she stayed as quiet as a mouse, barely drawing a breath.

"So, tell mc of this dream, Grandmother. Was it a true dream or no?"

"Well, I can't say," said the grandmother. "I dreamt of a golden-haired princess who roamed the world, hunting for her Raven sweetheart. But sadly, no matter how far she wandered she could not find him."

"Ah, it was a true dream then, for there is such a princess and she has wandered far looking for her sweetheart, just as you have said. Unlikely though she is to find him."

"Really? Why would you say so?"

"Because he lives in a castle, on an island in an endless sea, at the furthest edges of the earth."

"How unfortunate! I had hoped that she would find him. But you say there would be no way for her to reach him?"

"Only if she were to have my pale horse. He can travel faster than a wish and would get her to the seashore quickly enough."

"But that still leaves the endless sea for her to cross. Maybe she could find a boat to take her..."

"*Pfft*, there is no boat that can sail that sea! But at its edge is a gnarled old pine tree with a hat snagged in its branches. That hat belongs to the west wind and he has been long looking for it. If she were to have it, then perhaps he would take her across that great water. Now I'm off about my business, thank you for my dinner!"

"Of course, my dear. You are very welcome," Death's Grandmother replied. "Will your horse need feeding as well?"

"You need not mind him. I left him grazing in the wood next door where I am sure he will be content till I have need of him again."

With that, Aurelina heard the swish of a cloak and the opening and closing of a door and the air about her grew warmer again.

A moment after that, the door to her hiding place opened and the old woman's kind face peered in.

"So, there you are, my child. The pale horse waits in the wood next door, if you are stouthearted enough to ride him," said the old woman. "Mount on his back and tell him where you wish to go and he will take you there. Be steadfast and brave and you may yet find your sweetheart. Good luck!"

Aurelina thanked her and left.

Just next door to the hut there was a tall dark wood, exactly as the old woman had said. Aurelina searched resolutely through the trees despite the shivers that ran up and down her spine. Sure enough, she found Death's pale horse tethered to an old oak, grazing peacefully.

He was a fearsome beast, as pale as old bone. The glow of gravelights shone from his eyes and softly blowing nostrils. Despite her shaking hands, Aurelina resolutely took up the pale horse's reins and mounted upon his back. He stood quiet enough until she told him where she wished to go. Away he flew like a whirlwind and before she could catch her breath, he had her on the shore of the endless sea. She dismounted from his back, and away he sped towards his home.

The princess found the gnarled old pine tree that Death had mentioned not far from where the pale horse had left her. Snagged in its branches was a hat, just as Death had said there would be. All through the treetop birds flew, squabbling over the hat and generally making a huge hubbub.

Picking up a pebble, the princess waited and threw it in their midst just as they had tugged the hat free from the branches. With a indignant squawk, they dropped their prize and flew away.

Aurelina caught it, and as she did she saw a fair-faced man dancing along the dune towards her, setting the grasses asway and aflutter around him.

"My hat, my hat, my dear sweet princess you have finally found my hat!" He spun her around and kissed her cheek. His breath was warm and sweet.

"No need to tell me your wish for I have seen you wandering the world and heard you asking about a certain Great Black Raven. Take my hand, take my hand for I was always one with a soft heart for lovers," and with that he swept her up onto his back.

Away he flew. The tumultuous waves that sped beneath them tickled her tired toes and the sea spray kissed her chapped lips. Before long she stood on another shore with a long line of steps stretching up a rocky crag before her and the west wind's wishes for good luck still whispering in her ears.

Up the steps she climbed, her feet were as light as air because her journey was almost at an end. As she went, she wondered if her sweetheart was well, would he be surprised that she found him despite his dire prediction? Would he be as overjoyed to see her as she would be to see him? But that was the question, was it not? Would he be happy to see her after she had ignored his warning and betrayed his trust?

Her heart began to grow heavy with such thoughts. By the time she had neared the top of the stairs, her happiness had turned to doubt, and her feet had turned to lead.

When she reached the top, she found a grassy hill crowned by a lovely castle made up of airy spires as delicate as spun glass. She, by contrast, was as grubby as a beggar-maid, with her shoes full of holes and her once fine dress worn down to threads. Aurelina could not bring herself to go to the front door, but instead went round to where the servants would be.

Once there, she knocked and asked if there was any work for her to do. The servant who answered the door did not recognize his former mistress. But he was kind enough and told her that there was work to be had in the kitchen, if she was willing to work hard.

And so she did, scrubbing pots and carrying trays until her arms were sore. Eventually she found the one she had been searching for, for so long, but she still could not bring herself to go to him. Instead, she would sneak glances of her raven-haired love whenever she could, most often in the evening when cook would send her out into the kitchen garden to pick vegetables. It was at that same time every day that the Raven King would come out onto his balcony, to stare out across the sea.

Aurelina watches from afar

One day the cook caught her at it.

"Well, Missy, if you have time to be mooning about, then you have time to help others out!" she said and sent her to the steward so that she might help with the upstairs cleaning.

The steward looked disapprovingly at Aurelina's tattered self but sent her along anyway to help sweep the chambers and make the beds. That was how she found herself in the Raven King's bedchamber, staring at the rumpled bedsheets. Unable to help herself, she laid down, resting her head on his pillow. It was so soft, and brought to mind happier times when she and her sweetheart would talk and laugh in their castle of alabaster with its shining silver roofs. Truth be told, she would even be happy now to live in the crude little hut he had first brought her to, if only they were living in it together.

Yet, she still could not bring herself to reveal who she was, fearing that she would learn he no longer loved her. That truth would hurt her far worse than the loneliness of being so close to him, and him not knowing. It felt as though she were further away from him now than ever she had been while on her journey.

That night, when the Raven King went to lay down in his bed, he found a single hair, bright as spun gold, gleaming across his pillow. It pierced his heart like an arrow, for he missed his Aurelina and often wondered where she was out in the wide world.

He carefully wrapped the golden strand around the third finger of his left hand and fell asleep to dream of the smiling face of his lost love.

This went on for far longer than it should. But I suppose that is be expected, for people often are fools when the heart is involved.

One season passed into the next. Every day, Aurelina would sneak in to lay her head on the king's pillow and every night he would find a golden hair waiting him, which he would wrap around his finger with the others.

There did finally come a point where the Raven King decided things had gotten out of hand and a resolution was needed.

So, one morning he went out as he usually did, then after making sure there was no one there to witness his subterfuge, snuck back in to hide in his closet. Shortly after, he saw one of the servants come in to clean. Her back was to him, and her hair was caught up beneath a large handkerchief, but he could see that she wore a tattered dress that may have once been fine. Much to his surprise, she lay down on his bed and rested her head on his pillow with a sigh.

He waited for a moment, then silently crept out to look down on the sleeping woman's face. Her cheeks had been darkened by the sun and made rough by the wind, and the hand beneath her cheek was callused, but that did not stop him from recognizing his heart's one true desire.

Gently he brushed his hand over her head, drawing with it the hand-kerchief. A river of golden hair spread out across his pillow and his once bride-to-be, lost to him so long ago, opened her glorious eyes. Startled, she gasped and sat up.

"I truly did not think I would see you again in this life time," he said, a soft smile was on his lips. "Why did you hide yourself among the servants? Why did you not show yourself to me?"

"I was not sure if you would be happy to see me," she admitted. "I thought you may be mad at me for betraying your trust, and not heeding your warning."

"I was mad, for a time," he admitted. "But only because I was forced to leave you. I knew it was a risk to give you the napkin before we were wed in truth but even so, I would have you happy no matter the cost to myself. Yet you found me, which could have been no small feat. How did you manage such a thing?"

So, she told him of her travels and all that she had gone through to find him. He, in turn, finally told her the full extent of the curse that his step-mother, the dowager queen, had put him under so that he might never find a queen of his own. She had hoped that he would be forced to fly far away from his father's kingdom, which was exactly what had come to pass.

The princess then told him of how she had watched him from afar and laid her head on his pillow every morning after he had gone. He showed her the strands of hair that she had left behind which he had wrapped about his finger.

And in this telling all was made plain and what ever secrets or doubts there might have been between them where banished like ghosts. Finally the golden-haired princess and her raven king where reunited. The band of hair encircling the Raven King's finger became a solid band of gold and a matching one graced Aurelina's finger, and never again were they parted.

The Violet sister had been adding her threads as the Indigo sister was finishing her tale. Now, she sat back to look at their weaving.

"Look at what we have made, my sisters, so bright and beautiful. It reminds me of a tale I heard told a long time ago. While we wait for the rain to clear, let me tell you of the Rainbow Prince and the girl that he fell in love with. They called her Fairer-than-a-Fairy."

The Violet Sister's Tale

Fairer-than-a-fairy

Once upon a time there was a small kingdom that stood at the edge of a fairy wood. It was ruled by a good king and a good queen who were just and kind. They had been married for many years and were happy in all things save one, they had no children. They had almost given up hope when wonder of wonders they were blessed with a lovely baby girl.

The king and queen were overjoyed. The king, in particular, thought his daughter was the most perfect thing in the world. He loved her dearly and would tell all that would listen of her beauty, saying often that she was fairer than the Fairy Queen herself.

Now, it had never occurred to the good-natured monarch that his boasts might insult the Fairy Queen, bringing the hatred and jealousy of her court down on the little princess. But that is exactly what it did.

Not long after the little princess had turned seven years old, she was play-ing not far from the wood's edge one day, when the most handsome pony she had ever seen came dancing up to her from over the grassy meadow. He had fuzzy little ears, and a shaggy forelock that hung down over his face. He was so adorably round that she had no fear of him and was soon up on his back even though he had neither saddle nor bridle.

She quickly came to realize her mis-take for it was not a pony's back she had climbed onto, but a pooka's. Away the fairy horse raced, faster than fastest steed in her father's stable, straight into the fairy wood.

Away
the fairy horse raced faster than the fastest steed

Around trees and over briars they sped, until they reached a tiny pool, shining mirror bright in the darkness of the deep wood. There the pooka stopped, and lifting up his heels, tossed her neatly into the water where she quickly sank and was soon out of the sight of mortal man.

The pooka stood there for quite some time, considering her fate as he watched the ripples die away into stillness. He thought it sad. The little princess had been brave, for although she clutched at his mane fearfully, she had shed not a single tear as he had stolen her away.

But it wasn't to her death that he had carried her, for the little mirror pool was actually a doorway to faerie. And that is where she found herself, surrounded by a host of strange creatures. Whether fair or foul, they all looked on her with distaste.

"So this is the little mortal who is fairer than our queen," they jeered and mocked her, calling her "fairer-than-a-fairy" as they pulled her along.

They left her in the care of Lagree, the oldest of their tribe, who was known for her sly and subtle cruelty. She did not beat the little girl but instead set her to work, cleaning a house that would never stay clean and tending a fire that the old fairy warned must never go out. For if it did, the relighting of it would be so perilous a task that the princess would most likely not survive it.

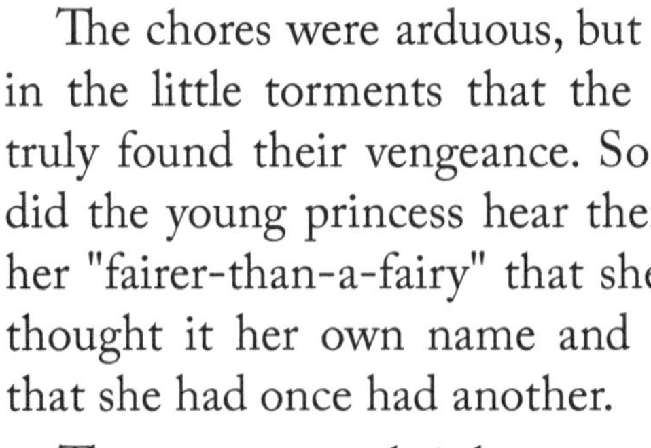

The chores were arduous, but it was in the little torments that the fairies truly found their vengeance. So often did the young princess hear them call her "fairer-than-a-fairy" that she soon thought it her own name and forgot that she had once had another.

There were two bright spots in her otherwise deary life. Two friends that came in the form of a sleek tom cat and a monstrous hound. They were her near constant companions, and whenever one was not at her side, then surely the other one could be found there. In their company, the other fairy's torments were less.

Many years passed, and the princess grew accustom to her lonely life. She obeyed the old Fairy's orders, and by degrees forgot all about the life she once had before.

One day, whilst in the courtyard sweeping the never ending dust that gathered on its flagstones, her eyes fell on the fountain in its center. The sun's light shone on it in just such a way so as to make the most brilliant rainbow. She stopped in her work, captivated by its dancing colors.

Wasn't she surprised when the rainbow spoke to her!

From the center of those vibrant hues came the most pleasant voice. It was that of a young man, and the words he used were so kind that for a moment she found she couldn't find any of her own to say back to him. It had been so long since anyone had spoken to her so gently that surely this was just a trick of her imagination. A fancy brought about by her loneliness, because there was no one visible in those bright colors.

Still, she answered the voice's greeting, for it had been long enough that she didn't care if it was her imagination. They talked long into the day. She learned that the voice belonged to the eldest son of a powerful king who had, quite unwittingly, angered the fairy, Lagree. Not being the forgiving sort, Lagree took her revenge by depriving him of his natural shape, imprisoning him in the form of a rainbow. If he still had a body, and what might have become to it, he had never known. Had, in fact, given up caring some time ago until he had caught a glimpse of Fairer-than-a-Fairy while she was going about her tasks. Since then, he had hoped she would look his way so that he might speak to her. And finally, that day had come. Now, he felt that his life once again held meaning.

His declaration touched her deeply, for she felt that in the Rainbow Prince, as she had begun to think of him, there was someone who could truly understand what she herself had endured. So, she shared all that had happened to her and what things she could remember from the life she had had before the one she now lived.

She had become so lost in the conversation that time slipped away from her. Thankfully, that was not so for her faithful friend, the cat. He nudged and bothered her until she realized that she was quite late in tending the fire. It was hard to say goodbye to the prince, but she promised to keep watch every day so that she might speak to him whenever the light fell on the water in just the right way.

It turned out that the cat's reminder was timely indeed, because when she went to check on the fire, it was nearly out. She carefully added oil to the basin and trimmed the wick, all without letting the flame die. When she was finished, she gently closed the lantern door to protect the flame from being blown out. That task completed, she began to shake, realizing how close to disaster she had come.

Even that could not deter her though. The next day, and every day there after, the princess went to the fountain. And whenever the sun shone brightly, she would find the Rainbow Prince waiting for her. They would talk for as long as the light lasted. Their friendship grew quickly, and over time it deepened, becoming something much more.

Now it was bound to happen, and so it did one fateful day. The princess lost track of time while she was talking to the Rainbow Prince, which in and of itself was not an uncommon thing. However, this time neither the cat nor the hound was there to remind her of her tasks and the fire which Lagree had charged her to care for, went out. Worst yet, it was Lagree herself who found the lantern, now dark and cold.

All the while, her lovely prisoner sat in the courtyard still talking to the Rainbow Prince, unaware of what had happened, until a dark shadow fell across the sparkling fountain. The rainbow's bright colors vanished. Fairer-than-a-Fairy turned to see Lagree standing there, a terrible glee gleaming in the old fairy's single eye. Then the princess saw the darkened lantern in her hand, and a cold shiver ran down her spine.

"So, this is where you have been lazing about! Well, we can't have that," Lagree said, but she didn't sound angry at all. In fact, she sounded almost happy as she reached out and easily cracked the fountain into pieces. The princess watched in horror as the water flowed away across the stones taking with it any chance she might have had to speak to her prince again.

"You let the fire die, and now you will have to relight it," the old fairy said, handing the lantern to young woman, "and only the ogre Locrinos has the flame you need for such a task.

"Ah, he so does find young meat the tenderest! But you would have to reach his house before worrying about that," Lagree continued, her one tooth glinting as she smiled her cruel smile. "Oh, the many interesting places you will have to travel through first. Every step through the Forest of Glass will cut your skin, and the Garden of Bells will drive you mad. So by the time you come to the Lake of Mirrors, well, you might welcome an end to your journey!"

"Then why should I go on the journey at all?" Fairer-than-a-Fairy asked. "As I see it, either way will prove an ill choice for me."

Old Lagree let out a terrible laugh.

"Because I put a *geas* on that lantern, foolish girl" she said. "As soon as your hand touched it, your fate was sealed. No matter what you do, you will have no choice but to continue your journey until the lantern is once again lit."

"And if I die in the trying?" the princess asked.

"Well at least I will be rid of you!" Lagree cackled, then left her, still chuckling.

Fairer-than-a-Fairy went back to the small closet where she slept and sat on the meager pallet which was her bed. And there for the first time since she had been stolen away, she wept.

That was how her friend the hound found her. He laid his head in her lap, and she gently stroked his ears.

"You know, it is not the journey that lies before me, nor its possible end, which makes me sad," she said, tears still wet on her cheeks. "It is that now the Rainbow Prince will be all alone again, and most likely will never know my fate. He will think I abandoned him. That is why I am crying."

"I do not doubt it," said a voice that she did not recognize.

When she looked down it wasn't the hound's monstrous head in her lap, but rather that of a youth who smiled up at her with pumpkin-orange eyes. She gasped and jumped up, leaving the young man stretched out on her bed.

"Who are you?" she exclaimed, and the youth sat up.

"Who am I? I have been your friend these many years. I am the hound that has lain at your feet, and the cat on your pillow who purred lullabies in your ear when sleep would not come," he replied. "I am also the pooka who stole you away, and for that I am truly sorry. But if you will trust me as you have so far, I hope to make amends."

The princess could not think of anything to say, but she cried all the harder, feeling as though she had not only lost her love, but her only friends as well, all in the same day.

The young man reached across to hold her hands, his eyes earnest and sad.

"I am sorry princess, and I swear since then I have done the best by you that I could. But Lagree is old and powerful. If she had seen me here, she would have banished me from your side, and you would have truly been alone!"

And it was true that she had rarely seen either the cat or the hound when the old fairy was at home.

"But now is not the time for tears," he insisted, and his eyes shined with mischief. "The way before you may look dark, but as you well know, looks can be deceiving. This doom may actually be a boon, before this story is over."

"How so?" she asked, hopeful despite herself.

"First let us fulfill this *geas*. To do that there are three things you will need: a pair of boots, a bag of cotton, and a hand mirror. All of which you can find in the bottom of a trunk that sits at the foot of the old fairy's bed. But how to get them, now that is sticky point."

"Perhaps not, if you are willing to help," she said, after some thought. "You know that she has only the one good tooth, which she has to keep in a strengthening potion every night. And that she takes it out in the morning to eat her breakfast. If you were to steal this from her, she would give chase for sure. Then I could sneak into her room and take what we need from the trunk with her none the wiser. She need never know.

When the morning came, Fairer-than-a-fairy woke and dressed, putting on every skirt she owned (of which there were only three), one on top of the other, then set forth on their plan.

The pooka waited patiently in his guise as a cat, and just as old Lagree was taking her tooth out of the potion, he leapt up and stole it right from her fingers. She gave chase as they had hoped. Once they were out of sight, the princess slipped into the cruel fairy's room.

There at the foot of the bed was a trunk and, in the bottom, just as the pooka had said, sat the boots, the bag of cotton, and the mirror. She carefully tied the boots and the bag under her skirts in just such a way so that they would not clank or sway, and in so doing give her away. Then she slipped the mirror in her bodice. She feared at first that it would be too big, but it seemed to grow smaller and smaller until it fit perfectly. She was back in the kitchen before Lagree had returned.

Shortly thereafter, the old fairy stamped into the kitchen, tooth in hand and very much annoyed. In fact, she was so annoyed she sent Fairer-than-a-Fairy off on her journey with barely a glance, save to give her the lantern, a jug of water, and a pocket full of hazelnuts.

Fairer-than-a-Fairy hurried off, concerned for the pooka whom she had last seen racing away with the stolen tooth. But she needn't have worried, for there he was, just a little ways down the road, a lovely black horse with wild pumpkin-orange eyes. She knew it was him, though he looked quite different from the shaggy-maned, round-bellied pony she remembered. He snorted at her and urged her to mount on his back. She did so, and away they went.

By midday, they stood at the edge of a wild wood made entirely of clear glass.

The princess slid from the pooka's back, and he was once more a man.

"The Forest of Glass," he said. "Some place you must go that I can not follow. But if you would heed my advice, I would say now is as good a time as any to put on those boots."

She sat down on the ground to follow the pooka's advice, for it seemed quite good advice to follow.

"One thing more," he said. "While in there look for two blooms you find pleasing to the eye, pluck them and bring them with you. They may prove useful before all of this tale is told."

With that, he promised to meet her on the other side of the wood, and turning himself into an eagle, he flew off. Once he had disappeared from sight, the princess made her way into the forest. Tall trees of cut glass spread their branches above her. Beneath them, brambles twisted themselves into tunnels through which she carefully slipped. Grass made of spun glass crunched loudly beneath her boots. Every leaf and stem she passed tore at her dress.

But she paid little mind to the danger because all around her rainbows danced, sparkling on every leaf, petal and blade of grass. They made her think of the Rainbow Prince. She wondered if he could see her even though she could not hear his voice in the colors surrounding her.

Plucking two glass roses from the arching canes above, she turned them this way and that, watching as the light fell through their prism of petals. She decided then and there that after she was free from her *geas* she would not go back to the fairy Lagree. Instead, she would set out to find her beloved, if he could be found.

She carefully removed her torn skirt, thankful that she wore two more beneath it, and wrapped the blooms. Tucking them safely in the bag of cotton, she continued on her way, finally coming out from the Forest of Glass. The pooka was waiting for her there, just as he said he would be. Mounting on his back, they headed off.

The sun was low on the horizon when the pooka stopped for the second time. The princess slid down from his back, and once again he stood beside her in the guise of a man.

"Up ahead is the Garden of Bells. Though you can not yet see it, if you listen carefully you can just hear it," he said, and when she listened closely, she could hear a faint sound on the wind. "Once again we come to some place you must go that I can not follow. But if you would keep the madness from your mind, then you must keep the sound of the bells from your ears. The cotton in your bag should do the trick."

"That is good advice that I shall be happy to heed, but there is a thing that I should tell you," Fairer-than-a-Fairy said as she pulled two pinches of cotton from her bag. "After I have seen this quest through, and my *geas* has lifted, I plan to continue on in search of the Rainbow Prince."

"Oh, and so I was sure you would," said the pooka and there was laughter in his voice, "for as I have said before, you are a brave girl to have weathered what you have without a tear or complaint. If that is to be your road, then one more suggestion I would make. The bells in this garden have many a virtue. So while you walk through, look for a bell that feels true to your heart. If you find one, bring it with you, for I am sure that it will be of some help before all is said and done."

With that he turned into an eagle once again and flew off. The princess stuffed the cotton in her ears and continued on her way. She soon came to a garden gate. Opening it, she went through.

The long light of the evening glinted throughout the garden on bells of every kind and size. They grew down from the trees and up from the ground in silver and gold and colored glass. Even bluebells grew here and there, who's tolling only dead men could hear. They all swayed gently, whether the breeze raced through them or not. But the tufts of cotton did their job well and she heard not a thing.

Though all were beautiful, with their delicate designs and jeweled clappers, there were none that stood out to her mind until she came to the gate at the very end of the garden. There hanging next to it was a plain brass bell. Seeing it filled her heart with such longing. Longing for a home that she had all but forgotten.

Stuffing more cotton from her bag around the clapper, she gently lifted it from its hook. She wrapped it in her second skirt and tied it tightly to her belt. Then passing through the gate, she hurried along the road to where the pooka waited for her, and away they went.

Night had already fallen by the time they reached the sandy shores of a waveless lake. The water stretched out, as still as a mirror, beneath the starry sky. A high-prowed boat, glowing with a soft pale light, sat quietly at its edge like a crescent moon come to earth. The sand shone like silver stardust beneath the pooka's hooves as they made their way towards the lake. He stopped just short of the water's edge and the princess slid from his back. In a blink he was there beside her, a pumpkin-orange eyed youth once more.

"Ah, the Lake of Mirrors. And there is our boat, waiting patiently," he said. "Fortunate, because you will have to cross it if you wish to reach the orge's house. Happily, this time I can come with you. Fair warning though, beautiful though it may be, this water is not for gazing into, lest you lose the whole of yourself in its reflection. So, take care to keep your eyes on the horizon."

With that warning in mind, they stepped lightly into the boat together, and it set off of its own accord.

They glided in silence across the lake, with only the stars to light their way.

Their eyes they kept fixed firmly on the horizon, so as not to fall to the temptation to look down into the water.

When they were almost half way across, Fairer-than-a-Fairy took out the jug of water, now near to empty, so that they might finish off what was left between them.

As she held the now empty jug, a thought came to her.

"Should I fill this with the water from here?" she wondered aloud.

"Not if it is to be for drinking, but if you had in mind for it another purpose, then perhaps it could prove useful."

She thought that having water that could capture one in its reflection, could indeed prove useful. But how to safely fill the jug, now that was the question!

It turned out to be a question that the pooka had an answer to. Because when she voiced it, he quickly reminded her of the little hand mirror she had taken from the old fairy's trunk.

She took it from her bodice, turning it just so, until the silvered water they glided across appeared in its surface. Looking only at the hand mirror, she carefully dipped the empty jug into the water, taking care not to touch it herself. When she felt she had enough, she pulled it up and corked it. Still looking away, she tore the hem of her dress to wipe the rim and all the places where the water might have touched.

"At this rate, I shall be unclothed before our quest is done!" she exclaimed. But when she looked she was glad she had, for the cloth now shined back at her as though it too was made of mirrored glass. She was careful not to look directly at it.

They landed on a rocky shore and left the boat glowing softly on the beach behind them. When scarcely a minute later she looked back, it was no where to be seen. Although a thin horned moon now rose in the sky just ahead of them to show them their way.

The pooka and Fairer-than-a-Fairy climbed up steep paths that wound and wound through rocky crags. In a very short time, a cottage appeared ahead of them. There they stopped and hid behind a huge boulder. They would need a plan if they were to get the fire and leave without the ogre using Fairer-than-a-Fairy's bones for toothpicks. Luckily, the pooka had already thought on just such a plan.

"We need only wait," he assured her. "Locrinos goes out most every night leaving his wife to sit at home. Although still an ogress, it is said she has a sweeter nature than her husband, and perhaps a gift may make it sweeter still. What do we have?"

They laid out all that they had from boots to bell and decided that the roses from the Forest of Glass would be the best gift.

"They are lovely, but I don't see why we need give her two when surely one will do," he said.

"I am glad you think so for the colors they cast in the light remind me of my love and I can't bring myself to part with both," Fairer-than-a-Fairy admitted. "But one I could give up, if it will soften the ogress's heart towards us."

While she spoke, she broke a rose from the stem, pricking herself on a glass thorn. Three drops of blood fell on its petals turning them deep red so that they shone like garnets, even in the thin light of the crescent moon.

"Hmm, better still," said the pooka. "But have a care to spill no more blood. We wouldn't wish to give her ideas." And with that, he took her finger and licked it. Just like that her skin was healed, as neat as you please.

They did not have to wait long before they saw the fearsome ogre leave the house, a sack thrown across his back. He gave his wife a kiss and left, hollering over his shoulder that he would be home before morning.

The two friends waited to make sure he was well and gone, before marching up and boldly knocking on the door.

The figure that opened it filled the doorway, but was not at all what one would have expected an ogress to look like. She was buxom and quite pretty, that is if one could ignore the small horns on her head and the fearsome tusks jutting up from her lips.

They greeted her most politely and told her that Lagree had sent them (which was the truth, after all), then showed her the darkened lantern.

They offered her the rose as a gift, just as they had planned, and she took great delight in it.

"Ah, mortal blood always smells the sweetest!" she sighed as she brought the garnet hued petals to her nose, gesturing for them to come in. "There is the fire, and you are welcome to it."

A giant hearth took up a whole corner of the cottage. Across the front of it were two doors made of metal and glass. When Fairer-than-a-Fairy bent to open them, she quickly learned that the fire they hid was of no ordinary flame. It burned with the same bright light as the sun, so that she could not look directly at it. The heat scorched her face and out of the corner of her eye, she could see the figures of salamanders dancing at the edges of the flames. She knew with absolute certainty that if she were to reach her hand in, it would be burned to the bone.

While she sat back on her heels, unsure of how she was to overcome this obstacle, she heard the pooka talking to the ogress. She realized that he was telling her of the Rainbow Prince, and Fairer-than-a-Fairy's love for him. Tears rose unbidden in her eyes, chasing themselves down her cheeks, and she was at a loss to stop them.

"Tsk, tsk, child," the Ogress tutted. "Such a waste!" and held a bowl beneath Fairer-than-a-Fairy's chin to catch the tears as they fell, only taking it away when it was near to brimming.

The Ogress dipped her finger in the bowl and tasted it, rolling her eyes to the heavens as though it were the most wondrous ambrosia.

"Umm, heartache and hopelessness! Such bitter tears do make the finest beer. My husband will be so happy! These are wonderful gifts you have given me, and I would give you some in return."

She handed the princess a long wand from a myrtle tree, and a small gray stone with a single band of white quartz circling its middle.

"The first will let you light the lantern if you can find a way to keep the salamanders from devouring it before you can gather the flame. The second is a wishing stone. Follow the path that continues beyond the cottage and it will bring you to a sea. When you are standing on the shore, hold the stone and make a wish, while tracing the path of quartz that circles it. Then throw it into the water. It will take you to your heart's desire."

Fairer-than-a-Fairy took the wand and the stone from the ogress. She put the stone in her pocket and when she did so felt the hazelnuts that were in there. Taking a handful out she tossed them into the hearth. The salamanders came to play with them and while the nuts crackled and popped, she reached in with the myrtle wand. The tip lit after a moment and she was able to light the lantern with it.

With that their quest was completed. She could feel the *geas* fall away like a collar from her neck. They bid the ogress goodbye, wishing her well in her beer making, and headed off down the path she had told them about. It wasn't long before they reached the sea. It stretched out in front of them, glittering beneath a blanket of stars. There they stopped and Fairer-than-a-Fairy took the wish stone from her pocket.

"You know with that stone you could return to the mortal realm, and Lagree would be none the wiser," the pooka pointed out.

"Truly, I could. But what good would it be if the Rainbow Prince wasn't there to share it with me. I have been gone twice on seven years, and I do not even know if there is a home to return to," she said. "And what of you, my friend? It was indeed a great harm you did when you stole me from my home, but your friendship over these many years has been a salve to my tortured heart. You owe me nothing more, yet still you seem ready to go on with me. What is it you seek for your future?"

"I don't know," the pooka admitted. "I find it best to read a story straight through and not to skip to the end. So let it be what it will be. But I have to say, I like sleeping on your feet and purring in your ear." That said, he turned himself into a cat and leapt to her shoulder where he tickled her cheek with his whiskers.

Choice made, she traced her finger along the ring of white quartz, and made her wish. Closing her eyes, she sent the stone sailing out over the water.

When next she opened her eyes, she found herself surrounded by huge trees. Thick silver chains hung down from their trunks, stretching like a glittering web across a small clearing. In its center was the most exquisite minute castle built entirely out of the palest alabaster. It sat about head height from the ground; rocking gently in its silver cradle as a sweet smelling wind whispered soothing lullabies through the evergreen needles above.

The princess and the pooka walked full round it ducking under the silver chains as they went. There were no windows to be seen, and only a single door without a knocker or a knob. There was, however, a bell pull beside the door, though there was no bell attached to it. Try as she might, the princess could see no way to reach it.

In the end, it was the pooka with the brass bell picked up on her journey clasped tightly between his teeth who climbed along the silver chains on his nimble cat feet. He placed the bell on the hook where it fitted as though it was meant to be there.

Once it was in place, Fairer-than-a-fairy pulled the bell chain, and the clapper, now free of its cotton wrapping, rang a pleasant chime. The knobless door opened. She climbed in, and the pooka hopped up readily after her. As soon as they crossed the threshold, the door closed quietly behind them.

The room they entered was pitch black, save for the light coming from the lantern in the princess's hand. It looked as though the whole of the castle was made up of a single room. The ceiling above them twinkled. On closer inspection, she found the whole of it set with jeweled planets surrounded by silver stars. Here and there gold comets flashed in the soft light.

There was no furniture to be seen, except an elegant couch around which rainbow-hued curtains hung; opaline specters swaying softly as the castle gently rocked like a boat on a calm sea.

A man lay reclining on the couch. When the princess approached him, she found that his eyes were open but seemed blind to all around him. She had no way of knowing if this was indeed her Rainbow Prince, but she thought him very handsome all the same. Of course, if he truly was the prince with whom she had been speaking with all these years, it would not have mattered how he had looked; she would have thought him handsome. For the heart sees the world differently, and through it, all things can become beautiful.

The pooka, a sleek black tomcat once more, jumped up onto the man's pillow and patted his cheek with a paw. The young man did not stir.

However, she had no time to wonder at this for there were more pressing concerns to attend to. She was quite sure that as soon as they had opened the door, the fairy Lagree would have known someone was at the castle. She was also sure that there would be a reckoning as soon as the old fairy caught up with them. Fortunately, a plan had been growing in her mind since they crossed the Lake of Mirrors.

She left the couch where the man lay, and setting the lantern in the middle of the room so that she might better see what she was about, crossed over to the door through which they had entered. There she took out the hand mirror which she had been carrying in her bodice, and propped it on the wall beside the door, angling it just so. To her surprise, it began to grow larger. It grew and grew until it stood on great golden feet, taller than she, and twice as wide.

She went next to the wall across from it and took out the jug which held the water from the Lake of Mirrors. Using the skirt which had once held the bell, she washed the wall until it too shone silver, careful to look only over her shoulder at the mirror she had propped up on the wall next to the door. When she was done, she left the jug and cloth in a corner; taking up the lantern once more, she went back to where the man lay. The cat still sat on the pillow beside his head, but now small red dots marred the prince's smooth cheek.

"Tsk, be careful you mean thing!" she scolded. "Why would you do that!"

"Because he hasn't said a thing," the pooka, human once again, groused from where he still sat on the pillow, poking the prince's cheek with his finger. "Can he not see you!"

"Is it such a wonder that he can't see me, trapped in a dark place as he is?" she asked. Carefully she unwrapped the glass rose, holding it up so that the radiant flame burning within the lantern could cast its light through it. A brilliant rainbow sprang from its petals and fell across the prince's eyes. His blind gaze cleared, and he turned to look at the princess who stood beside him. And although Fairer-than-a-Fairy, having never seen him in the flesh, had not been sure that he was indeed her Rainbow Prince, he certainly recognized her. A smile, bright as the summer sun, lit his face at the sight.

It was at that very moment that Lagree arrived. Flinging open the castle door, the wicked fairy saw the two young lovers surrounded by the lantern's light, a warm bright island amid a sea of darkness. With a howl of rage, she raced in straight away, reaching out with her cruel hands to grab them. This time, she would just throttle the life out of them and be done with it. But her hands closed on empty air, as though they were ghosts. There was no flesh beneath her bony fingers. She turned to go back the way she had come, but she found she couldn't.

And that, of course, was because it was not the two lovers themselves that she had seen. Rather it had been their reflections cast from the mirror that Fairer-than-a-Fairy had placed near to the door, onto the wall which she had painted with the waters from the lake. It was towards that very same mirrored wall that Lagree had rushed, intent on catching the two young lovers, only to be caught herself.

So there was nothing she could do as she watched Fairer-than-a-Fairy and her Rainbow Prince ran, hand in hand, out through the door. Nor was there anything she could do when the reflection of the cat who was with them winked one pumpkin-orange eye back at her as they left.

Once the three of them, the princess, the prince and the pooka, were free from the castle, they laughed and hugged each other happily. The castle door closed behind them, and they took the little brass bell from where it hung. As soon as they had, the whole castle seemed to melt, much to prince and princess's surprise. It became a tiny pool, shining mirror bright in the darkness of the deep wood. It was of course the very same pool in which the pooka had tossed the princess all those years ago.

"If you jump as far as you can out into the middle, you will come out the other side, back into your very own wood," the pooka told them.

Fairer-than-a-Fairy hugged her friend fiercely.

"Will you come with us? I am not sure what awaits me when I return home. But no matter what it is, it will better if you were there with me," the princess said sincerely for she held no ill will towards the pooka for having been the one to have stolen her away.

"Yes, please come with us," the prince added. "We would have been lost long ago had you not been a friend to Fairer-than-a-Fairy."

The pooka agreed, thinking it a fine idea to go and live in the mortal realm. Truth be told, he really did like sleeping on the princess's feet and purring in her ear. And he figured the beds at the castle would be much softer than the one they slept on at the old fairy's house. Having decided, he turned himself back into a fine black horse. The princess and prince climbed on his back and together they leapt into the mirror bright pool.

In the end, it turned out even better than anyone could have hoped. For it seems that time moves differently in faerie than it does in the mortal realm. So, it had been only fourteen months, not fourteen years since the princess had gone missing.

And though the king and queen were surprised to see their daughter now grown, with a suitor in tow no less, they were both so overjoyed to have her returned that they did not let such a thing bother them for very long. The king, who had been the saddest of all, could not have been happier, welcoming them all with open arms. Even the pumpkin-eyed cat who seemed to delight in shedding black hairs all over the castle's white pillows.

In time, the prince was reunited with his family, who it turned out lived just beyond the eastern sea; and they all gathered together to celebrate the joining of the two young lovers. They lived happily with their friends and family around them. Even as the years passed into decades, and they themselves became the rulers of their lands, time diminished neither the virtues, beauty, nor the mutual affection of King Rainbow and his Queen, Fairer-than-a-Fairy.

As Sister Violet finished her tale and the last knot besides, the rain faded over the horizon. The storm clouds had passed, and the sisters went out each holding an edge of what they had made together. Laughing, they chased after the retreating clouds, the colorful arc of their weaving filling the sky behind them.

Author's Notes

The Swan Maiden - I first read "The Swan Maiden" by Howard Pyle in this wonderful series of red books called *The Children's Hour* (Copyright 1969,1966 by Grolier Inc.) that I had found tucked away in my grandmama's house. I loved the idea of a young woman who could turn into a swan, a three eyed witch who lived in a house that shone like fire and the barley woman made of honey and barley meal. For some reason, these images captured my imagination as a child, and I returned to read about them again and again. Which probably explains why this retelling, out of all the other retellings in this book, comes closest to the original work. The orginal story first appeared in Pyle's book *The Wonder Clock*, published in 1887.

The Tiger Prince - I have a picture of my daughter, Lena, as a young girl sitting on the back of a great bronze tiger that we happened across at the zoo. Seeing it, how could I not picture a princess riding on the back of a huge tiger; a prince among tigers with a coat like living flame. From there, the story of *The Tiger Prince* grew, taking on a life of its own, as all good stories seem to.

The Fish Who Was Sometimes A Boy - Another story that started life as a picture taken while on an outing with my daughter. We were walking along a wooden walkway over a lake when I saw a flash of gold in the tea-colored water. Below was the most stunning koi fish. It kept appearing and disappearing in the weeds under the water. It was a brilliant gold, the kind of magical color that you can't help but try to keep a hold of, like rainbows and soap bubbles. Unfortunately, there was also an alligator that seemed intent on catching it. The golden koi disappeared for the last time into the weeds after a narrow escape, and from that moment The Golden Fish Scale (or The Fish Who Was Sometimes a Boy) grew. The young girl's name, Nobuko, was the name of a kind woman I remember from my childhood, and who will always hold a special place in my heart.

The Rocking Horse - Sometimes our memories paint the stories of our childhood so differently that I wonder if I am reading the same story at all! For me, the underlying theme of Housmans' Rocking Horse Land was so much changed between my reading of it as a child and my reading of it as an adult that my enjoyment of it dimmed a little. Well, I was looking at pictures I had taken at Christmas and one just jumped out at me. My daughter's old rocking horse "E" (short for E,I,E,I,O) was in that picture. He was a little worse for wear, having survived not just her childhood but a number of other children who, when over for a visit, would hug him and hang off his neck. Of course, he weathered all this attention with the stoicism that all well-loved toys do. And with that thought, a story popped into my head, heavily influenced by my memories of Laurence Housmans' Rocking Horse Land, but in many ways completely different it.

As for "E", I can't bring myself to let him go, so he is now a permeant decoration at Christmas. We had found him at Home Depot where he had already been broken by a couple of larger children who had used him roughly, so he came home with us. He was a rescue, like so many other things around my house.

Daughter of the Sea - This story came to me all in a flash one day while I was driving. There was a storm on the horizon. The sky was a riot of pewter and silver, and the wind was sharp and stinging. It was my favorite kind of day, and when I was younger I used to love going to the beach on gray days just like that one.

In retrospect, the story might have gotten some of its inspiration from "The White Horse of Volendam" another story I had found when I was young in the very same wonderful red books I mentioned previously.

The Raven's Bride - is a retelling of Howard Pyle's "Princess Golden-Hair and the Great Black Raven" which appeared in his book *The Wonder Clock* published in 1887. If you have ever read the original, you will find many of the elements changed in my telling of it; although I don't think I would go so far as to call it a reimagining. Whether you are a fan of the original or have never heard of it before in your life, I hope you enjoyed my telling of it.

Fairer-than-a-Fairy - I first read this story in Andrew Lang's *Yellow Fairy Book*, though apparently, the story was orginally published in 1718 as "Le Princ Arc-en-ciel". It was done so anonymously, but has often been attributed to the Chevalier de Mailly.

I will admit, I kept only a very few elements of the original story. However, this reimagining of mine is still the tale of a young woman's quest to rescue an imprisoned prince. I don't know about you, but I always enjoy a good quest!

www.ingramcontent.com/pod-product-compliance
Lightning Source LLC
Chambersburg PA
CBHW042104160726
48295CB00017B/986